Young Girl With Strange Powers

At fifteen, Anne became a prostitute. Her customers left her warm bed for a cold, unexpected—seemingly accidental—death.

The first man to seduce Anne was killed in a terrible auto crash—his legs were suddenly, mysteriously paralyzed, and he was unable to apply the car's brakes. Police reports showed the cause of death as a heart attack. Anne walked away from the accident unhurt and unseen.

The first woman to seduce Anne later shot her own husband, and then put the shotgun into her mouth and pulled the trigger. Anne left town unnoticed.

WHO WOULD BE NEXT?

CHARLES W. RUNYON

Soulmate

AVON
PUBLISHERS OF BARD, CAMELOT, DISCUS, EQUINOX AND FLARE BOOKS

SOULMATE is an original publication of Avon Books.
This work has never before appeared in any form.

AVON BOOKS
A division of
The Hearst Corporation
959 Eighth Avenue
New York, New York 10019

Copyright © 1974 by Charles W. Runyon.
Published by arrangement with the author.

All rights reserved, which includes the right
to reproduce this book or portions thereof in
any form whatsoever. For information address
Scott Meredith Literary Agency, Inc.,
580 Fifth Avenue, New York, New York 10036.

First Avon Printing, March, 1974.

AVON TRADEMARK REG. U.S. PAT. OFF. AND
FOREIGN COUNTRIES, REGISTERED TRADEMARK—
MARCA REGISTRADA, HECHO EN CHICAGO, U.S.A.

Printed in the U.S.A.

ONE

ANNE had never been close to anything completely and consciously Evil. She'd seen boys kill birds with bb guns, she'd seen playground bullies beat up younger kids, she had even, once, seen a car swerve to strike down a land tortoise creeping slowly across the road in the early springtime, and her stomach had sickened at the sight of the split shell and the body pulped to a red splash. But none of these things, though they had been unpleasant, cruel, and even sadistic, had been Evil. Nor had they been directed at her.

The underground room was cool and pungent with the smell of ancient dust. The thick stone walls held a tiny pocket of silence, and the feminine voice of the tour guide was dim and distant as a memory: "The palisade construction is typical of frontier forts built during the eighteen-fifties . . . ."

Anne felt an urge to climb back up the steps, to the stinging heat of the August sun, the smells of melting creosote and the familiar faces of her parents and brother. But fascination held her, one foot on the earthen floor of the chamber, the other bent backward with toe resting on the bottom step, her eyes fixed on the corner between the roof beams. Up there was a black, wet, shiny substance about the size of an outspread hand. Around it spread a band of transparent gelatin which mirrored the room: beams, cobwebs, the gray stone walls, the steps, her own broomstick body with short white dress and patent-leather shoes—all were sharpened, reduced, fattened at the middle, and elongated at top and bottom. It was like staring into a gigantic eyeball.

Anne felt pressure against her forehead. The black lens was moving, swelling up to the size of a dinner plate, sending out little feelers, black as ink but glowing around the edge. One tentacle dropped down and sped along the dirt toward her. She gasped and lifted her foot onto the step. The thing meant to destroy her—not impersonally, like a lightning bolt, or like a snake which strikes by instinct unable to see. She felt as if it knew her to the depth of her soul and hated what it knew. She turned and ran up the steps, only to collide with the stocky form of her brother.

"Hey, what's the matter?"

She tried to go around him but he blocked her, casually, out of habit. "Look up . . . up in the corner," she gasped. "Billy, let me *past!*"

"Wait a sec." He jumped down into the room and stood with fists jammed against his hips. He was fourteen, three years older than Anne, with a swirl of thick taffy hair topping a heavy body still smooth with the tallow of baby fat. His hand held a short, pointed stick. His snub nose wrinkled, his upper lip lifted up and out, giving him a strong and wilful look. Anne saw that the thing had withdrawn its tentacle and shrunk to the size of a teacup, no longer black but a cool blue tinged with scarlet, shot with flashes of angry red. She felt her stomach knot with fear as Billy attacked the lens, holding the pointed stick in both hands, stabbing and stabbing until the breath hissed between his teeth. A tentacle lashed out, recoiled, lashed out again. Billy gave a shout of triumph and made a bent-over scurry across the room. "Got it!" He raised a lizard and swung it by the tail. Blood dripped off its nose; the head hung at an angle, nearly severed from the long mottled body. The legs were trembling as they froze into rigidity. Her brother grinned, his eyes alight but narrow. "Sonofabitch, tried to bite me."

Anne glanced up at the corner; the thing was gone. She bent and gazed into the lizard's eye, then drew back with a gasp. The thing had somehow gone into the body of the lizard; she saw it coiled up inside, and felt the hot sour thrust of its hatred. "It's alive."

"Aw, how can it be? Look, the head's almost cut off."

"It's alive. Look at its eye."

"You look. Here!"

He swung it toward her; blood flew out and stitched the front of her dress with red droplets. Anne screamed and jumped back. Billy laughed and advanced toward her, holding the creature out at arm's length.

"What are you kids doing?"

Anne's mother stood halfway down the steps, eyes wide against the darkness. She had Anne's features: eyes big and heavily-lashed, the skin around them clay-gray and dusted with brown freckles, nose long and high in the bridge, with a dent on each side as if someone had pinched it between thumb and forefinger, and twisted. But where Anne's thin, knobby frame made these features grotesque, her mother's mature body blended them into a pleasant face of strong character. The vague surprise in her eyes came from the fact that she was myopic, and too concerned with the appearance of youth to wear glasses. Now she squinted, leaning forward to see what Billy held. Seeing the shape of his trophy, she recoiled, placing her palm flat against the stone wall to keep her balance. "Oh God! Throw it down, Billy!"

"I'm gonna take it home and pickle it in a jar, like Chris did his appendix."

"You certainly are not."

"Dad won't care. I'm gonna go ask him."

Billy was gone, taking the steps two at a time. Anne's mother recoiled as he passed, her eyes on the dead animal. Then she looked at Anne. There was contact, more than mother-daughter, a unity of sex. They had the understanding of two women in a household containing two aggressive, demanding males. "You want to go up, Anne? She's telling about the massacre."

"All right."

The sky glared like a molten mirror. The sudden heat made Anne sneeze. The crunch of her shiny shoes on the gravel sounded strange and unreal to her ears.

"The Indians apparently entered by digging under the walls . . . ."

Anne peered between two spectators at the park service guide. She wore a tight blouse and short skirt of tailored seersucker, and her blonde hair hung to her shoulders like a kepi. Anne felt envy and admiration; the woman was beautiful, with a straight narrow nose and skin that glowed like a polished apple.

". . . . None of the soldiers survived; most of them were murdered in their sleep. They'd probably neglected to post enough guards, since the fort was supposed to be impregnable . . . ."

"Like the Maginot line," said Anne's father. He stood half a head taller than the other men in the group, holding his pipe between his teeth, his index finger hooked around the shank, elbow resting in the cupped palm of his other hand. A self-confident man, with square shoulders and dark blond hair; Anne wanted to go over and take his hand and let the others know he was her father.

The woman smiled. "Well, yes. More or less. Apparently the women were carried off to serve as slaves . . . or whatever use the Indians might make of them." Her eyes flicked over to Anne's father's, and her tongue-tip slid across her lower lip. "They also carried off their dead, if there were any. The Indians believed that to leave a slain warrior on the battlefield was to condemn his soul." The woman folded her arms beneath her breasts, pushing them up and out against her blouse, and even from a low angle Anne could see the deep blue-veined rift between them. The woman had her back against the wall, thrusting her hips forward and tilting her pelvis up. It seemed normal to Anne; older girls at school stood that why when they talked to boys. What caught her eye was the black luminous line which vibrated around the woman. It was the same light she'd seen around the lizard.

Her mother's hand slid into hers and pulled her gently away. They walked to a low parapet and stood, hips touching, looking across the wooded valley. Anne said: "She *is* beautiful, isn't she?"

"Yes. Like a cobra." The corners of her mother's mouth turned down, making her face harsh and craggy. Then the harshness melted, leaving only a tired look of age. "He's old enough to look out for himself, Anne. Let's sit in the car."

A breeze blew through the open car doors, stirring the wisps of ashen hair on her mother's neck. Anne watched her open her purse and take out a pack of cigarettes. The rustle of cellophane sounded harsh and loud, like somebody stepping on a basket. The snap of her mother's cigarette lighter was like the clatter of the spring-latch on the garage door. Anne felt jumpy and nervous; she wanted to scream but could think of no reason to do so.

People started shuffling out of the fort. Shoes grated on gravel, starters whirred, dust spewed from rear tires. The last to appear was Billy, carrying a paper bag. He said "Hi!" and opened the back door.

"Have you got that lizard in there?" asked Anne.

"No." Billy grinned.

"Open it and let me see."

"Try and get it open."

"I'm not riding home with a dead lizard."

"Walkin' ain't crowded."

"God! Will you children—? Billy, where's your father?"

"I dunno. Inside."

The only cars left were theirs and a yellow Cougar. Anne knew somehow that it belonged to the park service guide. Her mother was holding the cigarette between her fingers and clicking her nails, a gesture which always made her husband grunt and shift his shoulders like a football player. Anne stepped out of the car. "I'll get him, Mama."

"Anne, you can't—

But Anne was running, the tips of her shoes kicking up spurts of gravel. She went into the long barren room where they sold souvenirs from a glass case. The case was locked, the rack of picture postcards unattended. Behind the counter was a door, above it a plastic sign lettered to look like chunks of wood. Holding her breath, Anne tapped a knuckle on the door: "Daddy, we're ready to go."

There was a long pause, then her father's mutter: "Wait in the car. Be right out."

Anne bit her tongue and crossed her fingers. "Mama said to wait and come back with you."

"Oh for God's sake. Go on. I'll be right behind you."

Anne scraped her feet across the floor, then tiptoed back and stood behind the postcard rack. A couple of minutes later her father stepped out of the office and walked to the outer door without glancing around. Outside he paused to comb his hair, then wiped the comb on his trousers like a barber stropping his razor, flick-flick. Through the window

Anne watched him shuffle across the lot, his head down, shoes scraping the gravel.

Anne planned to walk quickly past the half-open door of the office, but she noticed something strange at the edge of her vision—a black inkblot shape sprawled on the red leatherette couch. It seemed to pulsate like a huge bladder, almost filling the room, then shrinking down to the size of a beach ball. Within the mass floated a ring of clear gelatine, with a now-familiar black lens inside it, glaring at Anne with a terrible loathing. Her step faltered, her legs turned to rope, and panic flapped its choking wings in her throat. She was about to fall when the thing spoke:

"What do you want, girl?"

Suddenly there was no black shape on the couch, only the park service guide lying naked on her back. Her incredible breasts defied gravity to stand almost upright on her chest. Below the flat stomach rose the pubic bush, thick, blonde and glossy, a proud adornment which made Anne envious. She wanted to touch it, and the thought made her skin tingle. She wanted to run, but for the second time that day fascination held her rooted.

"The thing in the underground room—are you part of it?"

"Am I part of it? Am I part of what?" The woman repeated it, like a child trying to understand. Anne saw a knife-edge of darkness appear around the white body. The woman seemed to vibrate. Her cheeks took on a waxy hue, her eyes changed to an electric, inhuman shade of blue, the hair became slick and glossy, like spun nylon. *She was a doll.* But the eyes were those of a real little girl, staring at Anne with fear and bewilderment. The doll-mouth gaped in what looked like a scream, but no sound came out. Anne felt a hot heaviness, as if a cinder cloud were billowing up around her, and the girl faded back into a dark cavern . . . .

Anne turned and ran, hitting the door with both hands. Halfway across the lot she tripped on her own feet and sprawled on the gravel. She heard the crunch of footsteps and tried to crawl away, but it was only her father. He picked her up and set her on her feet, then he knelt down and brushed away the pebbles which had gouged her knees. She saw the bald spot on his crown and realized he was getting old. She pictured him lying dead in a coffin, herself dry-eyed, unable to express her grief.

"Come on now," he said, rising and sliding his arm around her shoulders. "We'll just forget about what you saw in there, won't we?"

She felt reassured by the man-tobacco smell of him, the sweat of his body. "I'll forget if that's what you want—but what was it?"

"It?" He looked at her in non-comprehension. "It . . . she's a woman, Anne. Not the best kind of woman, but . . . ." His hand moved gently forward. "Let's not talk about it anymore, huh?"

As they walked, her father's arm across her shoulders, Anne glanced back at the doorway. A blue glow seemed to rise from within; now there was malevolent hatred and a hazy warping of the air around it. Anne shivered and drew away from her father. She felt cold and alone.

The feeling stayed during the ride home. She asked Billy what he'd done with the lizard, and he said: "I put it in the trunk. Daddy said I could, didn't you, Daddy? Tell her."

Her father's eyes met hers in the rear view mirror then slid away; his voice sounded tired. "He's just going to show it around, then throw it away." He drove a minute, frowning to himself. "It's a leopard lizard, native of the desert."

"It's a long way from home," said Anne.

"Well, it's what they call an anomaly. Animals out of their natural habitat. But . . . ." He frowned, as though he'd lost his train of thought, then picked it up again. "But those things happen." He was still frowning as he plucked a flake of tobacco off his lower lip.

"Did you like the fort, John?" Her mother's voice was crisp and polite.

"Yes, it was very interesting."

"I'm sure it must have been. There's a long blonde hair on your shoulder."

"Oh Christ. And that's supposed to mean something?"

"No, it doesn't mean anything. Nothing means anything."

Home. Billy went out with his trophy. Daddy took a couple of pills and went to bed, his ruddy face blotched with pallor. Mama mixed a martini and started taking a bath. Anne fed her hamsters and watered her azalea then went upstairs to her room. She looked down the sloping lawn to the water, where a motorboat nosed against a wooden jetty. Across the narrow cove, the Blyth's colonial home reared up from behind a screen of poplars. Anne thought of going over to tell Janet about the thing in the underground room, and the naked woman in the office. She decided to wait until dark, when Janet would find it easier to believe. Anne lay down and listened to the faint sound of her mother's voice rising from her parents' bedroom. It started out pleasant and casual, then gradually tightened to a spiteful twang. Daddy's response was a low mutter, trailing off into silence. Strange. Usually he shut her up with a bark.

Anne folded her hands behind her head and closed her eyes. Supper would be late tonight; Mama would be puffy-eyed and trembly. There would be too much salt on the potatoes and no vinegar on the spinach . . . .

She woke up sweating. The heavy smell in the room reminded her of the time she'd found the withered corpse of her cat under a rosebush. Something dead. Very close. She reached back to plump her pillow and touched something cool, with the solidity of flesh. She sat up like an uncoiling spring and jerked away the pillow. The dead lizard. The damn kid had put it under her pillow! She jumped out on the floor and waited for the flood of revulsion. Nothing. Not even anger at Billy, just a quiet exasperation. He was a child.

The dead flesh had congealed into a half-circle. She picked it up by the tail and held it in front of her. "Are you dead, finally?" The filmed eyes gave her the answer. Carrying the little corpse, she went across the hall. Billy's room was empty. Downstairs, the TV played to a vacant chair. She went into the kitchen and crammed the lizard into the garbage disposal unit, shivering with delight at the juicy crackle of chewed flesh and bones. At last it was gone, and she could forget the fort and its horrors.

She turned away thoughtfully and went out on the porch. It was getting dark, but the things she'd planned to tell Janet no longer seemed important. What was important? She didn't know, but she felt the moment stretch like a rubber band; her heart beat faster, her stomach fluttered as though she were on a roller coaster about to drop—

"Anne! Anne!"

She ran to her parents' bedroom and threw open the door. Her mother stood beside the bed, her face flushed and pouchy, trying to hold her robe together with one hand and push the hair out of her eyes with the other. Daddy lay on his back . . . asleep? Not asleep. His eyes were open, staring at the ceiling.

"We were—he was talking to me and he just rolled up his eyes and . . . and *died!*"

TWO

GRANDPA, with his jacket off and his necktie loosened, was saying: "You'd think they'd put down something besides 'Cause undetermined'. Heart failure, maybe."

Grandma, sitting in the front seat on the other side of Anne, said: "If they don't know they don't know, Maynard. Look Anne, there's the place we had hamburgers when you and Billy came down last summer."

Anne nodded. "I'd like some now."

"But you just—" Grandpa caught himself, and stepped on the brake. "You eat as often as you want, Anne. I'll stop every five miles if you say the word."

As she chewed her third hamburger, with ketchup and relish and a side order of french-fries, Anne thought about her mother. In the two days since Daddy's death she had felt further and further away from her. Anne had tried to tell her about the woman, but Mama wouldn't listen. "He was an exciting man, Anne. He lived as if each day were his last—and finally, it was." Anne wondered if she'd ever see her again, or Billy, who was leaving for camp the next day. She recalled the funny, poetic way Mama had said goodbye: "I've got to be alone for awhile, feel the wind in my face, learn to live without the shelter of a strong man." Anne had kissed her dry lips with the feeling that it was for the last time.

The farm was eighty acres, one mile off the superhighway, on a gravel road. Grandpa pulled up in front of the cottage, built of locally quarried granite.

"Built it with these," he said, holding his hands out from the wheel. Either of them was big enough to hold a basketball from the top.

Within minutes Grandma had her apron on and was filling the house with odors of fried chicken, dressing, mashed potatoes, string beans, home-baked biscuits, apple pie and chocolate cake. Grandma was small and round, her once-auburn hair faded to the color of beeswax. She widened her eyes in mock surprise as Anne filled her plate for the third time. "I can't believe you're the same girl who stayed with us last summer. You ate so little I was afraid you'd blow away in the high wind."

That night there was fresh-churned butter, home-baked bread, meat loaf and cottage cheese. Grandpa lifted his bushy eyebrows as the last chunk of meat loaf went onto Anne's plate. "Keep on that way and you'll be able to wear my shoes." Anne laughed, because his feet were so enormous he had to wear tennis shoes with slits cut in the sides.

But Anne wondered. Was she growing? The food filled her stomach only a little while; the next hour she was always hungry. During the next three meals she ate until there was nothing left on the table, and the two dogs and five cats were forced to eat the commercial gruel which Grandma made up for them. Even so, a raging appetite forced Anne to get out of bed at ten p.m. and clean out the icebox. At midnight she was awakened by a dream of sizzling steaks and endless serrated rows of chocolate fudge with walnuts on top. The icebox was bare, so she went outdoors in her bare feet and short night dress. The weathercock on top of the barn caught the moonlight and turned itself into a fabulous silver bird. Anne stopped for a moment, caught by the feeling that the barn, the maple trees, the spyrea beside the cellar were all aspects of an alien place, as strange and distant as the moons of Jupiter. A knifing cramp in her stomach nudged her mind back to food. She lifted the slanted door of the cellar and walked down into the warm darkness. Her nose caught the pungent fragrance of apples. She found the bin by smell, lifted out an apple and bit in. The crackly-pulpy sound of her eating reminded her of the noise the lizard had made in the garbage disposal. Five apples took the edge off her hunger, and she moved to the rows of jars which filled the shelves. She seized one, jerked out the rubber ring, and twisted off the cap. She fingered out a round object and stuck it in her mouth. Pickled beets. She ate the whole jar and drank the juice, feeling it run down her chin and onto her nightdress. She reached for another, and Grandpa's voice boomed: "Come outa there with your hands up!"

The jar crashed on the floor, the juice spattered her legs. Anne stepped over the broken glass and walked out. Grandpa stood at the top of the steps with a shotgun. He breathed, "Good God," and swung the gun away. "What were you doing down there, Anne?"

"I got hungry, Grandpa."

"Holy Jesus," he said.

Grandma was up by now, her lips pursed with concern. She filled the tub so Anne could wash off the beet juice, then loaned her a flannel nightgown and tucked her in bed. Anne could hear their mumbled conversation for a long time, then the growling of her stomach interfered. She'd have to find a way to get food without anybody knowing. She decided to take the fifty dollars Mama had given her and hitch-hike to town. She'd buy a box of groceries and hide them in the back pasture . . . .

Next morning, as she ate her third stack of pancakes with butter and maple syrup, she heard Grandma on the phone: " . . . tapeworms? I just wondered if she'd been to the doctor recently?" Silence, then: "Well, we'll take her for a checkup this morning. No need for you to come down, we enjoy taking care of someone. How does Billy like camp? That's good . . . ."

The clinic was embarrassing. After a sweaty effort in the clinic bathroom, Anne managed to produce stool and urine samples. The doctor was young, with moustache and full sideburns fluffing out along his jaws. He poked and prodded her stomach and held a stethoscope to her flat chest. His touch excited her; he was the first man outside her family to touch her skin where it was normally covered by clothing. After she got dressed he talked to them all in his office: "Eleven, you said? She seems to be maturing early, but there's nothing to worry about, unless the lab turns up something I don't expect. You have a very healthy granddaughter here, and the excessive appetite is just part of the growth process."

His words ended the worry, and Grandpa even laughed in the drug store when she ordered a third malted milk. They argued awhile when she asked to stay in town and take a taxi home, but they finally gave in. She was, after all, maturing early. . . .

She had the taxi let her off on the dirt road which ran along the back pasture. She shouldered the box of groceries, climbed a small hill and went down into a wooded valley patched with hickory and scrub oaks. At the head of the valley was Grandpa's pond, fed by a spring which kept the water clear. On this hot August afternoon, two Jersey milk cows stood in water up to their udders, switching their tails and chewing their cuds. Anne pondered: Where could she hide the groceries so they wouldn't be stepped on and scattered? Below the pond was a slew covered by four inches of warm stagnant water. Saw grass and cattails grew higher than her head, and she sank to her calves in the muck. She found a stack of half-cut granite blocks where Grandpa had quarried rock for the house; on the top of a large boulder she built a shelter of granite chips and stowed the food inside. Her dress clung to her waist, sodden with sweat. The sun beamed down and gnats clung to her nose and ears, while mosquitos pierced her skin. Climbing up to the pond, she took off her dress and waded in. The water was warm on top, but near the graveled bottom it was cool. She swam for a few minutes, then climbed out and lay down on her dress, waiting for the sun to dry her. Maturing early, the doctor had said. Was that true? She raised herself on her elbows and looked down her body; the buds of her breasts were the size of acorns, changing color from pale beige to bruised pink. She remembered Thelma, a neighborhood girl who'd gone away to camp one summer and returned with breasts the size of teacups. But Thelma was thirteen when that happened; Anne was barely eleven. Still they seemed larger than yesterday, and they were certainly tender . . . .

Next afternoon when she took her swim, she noticed that two faint mounds had risen on her chest, half a handspan across. The day after that they'd grown big enough to cast a shadow, and a wisp of dark red hair had appeared on the barren hump of her pubic mount. Did it happen so fast? Anne didn't know, and there was nobody she dared to ask.

By the end of the week she'd begun to outgrow her clothing. Her money was gone, having been spent in two more trips to town for groceries. She borrowed one of Grandpa's denim shirts, liking the smell of his pipe and the sun which clung to the fabric—but wary of the way his eyes followed the bounce of flesh beneath it. By now she could barely cup her hands over her breasts. Her jeans were impossibly tight across her hips, even when she left the zipper open. She asked her grandmother to teach her sewing.

That night Anne sat in the kitchen with the sewing machine on the table, trying to make a dress which would encompass her blooming body. She could hear bits of conversation from the living room, while her grandfather tuned the TV.

" . . . turn for the better, young woman interested in sewing and cooking."

"Anne isn't a young woman," said Anne's grandmother. "She's an eleven-year-old child."

". . . maturing earlier these days. In my day you'd never see bumpers like that on a schoolgirl."

"Maynard! Your own flesh and . . . ."

". . . Man reaches sixty-five he doesn't necessarily go blind . . . . "

" . . . the same I wonder if there might be something wrong with her glands. I think we'd better . . . . "

Theme music came up and drowned out the voices. Discovery was something to be avoided; Anne wasn't sure why. She'd begun to realize that her sudden growth might make it impossible to go back to her old life, and the thought brought a flutter of panic.

She went into the bathroom and looked at herself in the mirror. Growth had not been confined to her body. Her hair was longer by at least a foot; now it hung half-way down her back in silky waves. It looked black as velvet, but when she lifted it into the light she perseived the red-purple highlights. Her eyes seemed grave and mature beneath a broad intelligent forehead—not the huge idiot saucers they'd once been. And that stupid nose—you could tell it was the same, but it was as though some magic surgeon had raised her cheekbones and smoothed out her chin and lower jaws. The face was a gentle oval, the nose merely prominent, and the new fullness of her lips covered her buck teeth. The effect was to give her a sultry, sensuous pout. Lying in bed later she thought: *I'm becoming a beautiful woman.* That made the future not half so scary.

She felt exhilarated next day at the pond. The soft breeze caressed her body as she waded in; little bubbles went plink-plink as the water seeped into her thick pubic mat. She leaned forward, feeling the buoyancy of her breasts, enjoying the way her nipples broke the water like the noses of two beavers swimming. A frog climbed out on the bank and jumped into the weeds, trailing a clear jet of water. She climbed out and ran after it, parting the tall grass with her hands. Suddenly she stopped and stood frozen.

A figure sat in a little bower made of saw grass bent over and woven at the top like a duck-blind. A man . . . or was it a man? His hair stood up in back like a cockatoo's crest, and a wiry growth of beard grew almost to his eyes. He looked like the pictures of satyrs who ran through the woods with naked women slung over their shoulders. She glanced toward his feet, but one was folded under him, or buried in the mud, or . . . . Her ears lay back as the truth struck her. He had only one leg. And his left arm ended in a steel claw. She saw the knife in his other hand and opened her mouth to scream.

Yet she couldn't believe that he'd come to attack her, though she'd read about such things in the papers. No. He dropped the knife and held up his hand. He wanted her to . . . what? Take his hand? His eyes burned into hers. His mouth opened, but he said nothing.

She saw as he raised his chin that there was no beard beneath his jaw, only a deep cleft and the slickness of scar tissue. He'd been hurt terribly—but not recently. She could see the memory of pain in his eyes, the fear of more pain. Silently she reached out and touched his fingers; perhaps it was the knowledge that this was a strange man and she was naked, but her fingers crackled with electricity. She felt her legs go soft and her nipples draw into a painful tightness.

The feeling scared her. She turned and ran, grabbing up her clothes as she fled. Halfway across the pasture she stopped and pulled on the blue jeans and shirt. She realized then that he could not have chased her on one leg, and was probably harmless.

She thought of him as she lay in bed that night, seeing the pain in his eyes and remembering the shock of his touch. His bower was empty when she went out the next day, but inside the stone hut where she kept her food she found two carved wooden figures. One showed herself as a young girl with narrow hips and thin legs and a long nose. The wood had turned brown from exposure to the air. The other figure had the slick whiteness of fresh carving. The breasts were cones of absolute perfection. The hips and buttocks were smoothly rounded, the thighs tapered gently to knee, then swelled out in the calf. The face was hers.

She felt a chill. He knew that she'd been changing rapidly. Maybe he was a wizard, making these dolls to cast a spell on her. But she didn't really like that idea. They were love gifts. He'd be there tomorrow. And she'd learn what had damaged his body so terribly, and why, despite his repulsive appearance, the touch of his hand sent an electric shock through her body.

She went home without taking her usual swim. Grandma and Grandpa waited in the kitchen with grave faces. Grandpa cleared his throat: "Your mother is coming down tomorrow morning. We've decided you're not normal, and so—"

Grandma gave him a look of disgust. "He means there's something strange about your development, and we think you should see a specialist. Later we want you to come back and live with us . . . . "

Anne had one dress fit to wear. The garment which had come to mid-thigh ten days ago now barely covered her buttocks, but they were wearing them short this summer anyway. By cutting the seams under her arms, she gave herself room to breathe.

She took Grandma's shawl of brown wool, supposedly hand-knitted in Ireland, put a few cans of food and a change of clothing in her cardboard suitcase—the two carved figures she tied up in the shawl—and at one-twenty a.m. left the house. She took the lane behind the barn and cut across the south pasture. The air felt heavy against her cheek; there were rumbles of thunder and flickers of lightning in the southwest.

The storm broke as she was climbing the fence. A gust of wind whipped up her skirt and snagged it on the barbed wire. She lost her balance and fell, gouging her thigh and ripping a huge triangle out of the back of her skirt. Rain slanted down in heavy drops, ten of which would have filled a teacup. She picked up the suitcase and walked into the wind; her face burned with excitement, it almost seemed that the water should sizzle against her skin. A half-dozen black cows huddled in a grove of trees, heads hanging low, letting the rain hammer down on their backs. The sod was spongy with moisture; in a short time her shoes were soaked. Already too tight, they shrank, the threads broke, and the seams parted. She sank into the mud, her shoes stayed while her feet moved on. She didn't bother going back.

She found the little creek out of its banks, a curling torrent of muddy water. She waded in, felt the current pull at her knees, then her hips; suddenly the weight of water swept her off her feet. She spun around and ducked under the icy water, then regained her footing and crawled out on the other side. The suitcase seemed impossibly light. She saw that the composition substance had torn like wet pie dough and dumped all her possessions into the stream. She tossed away the handle and plodded on. The shawl was a sodden weight on her shoulders. She wrung it out and discovered that the woman-figure had been lost. She wrapped the remaining figure securely and tied it around her waist. A few minutes later a six-foot steel-mesh fence blocked her path. Beyond it, at the bottom of a steep embankment, she saw the asphalt ribbon of the highway shrouded in a fog of raindrops. She hooked her toes between the links and climbed the fence, then straddled the three strands of barbed wire. Finding no toehold on the other side, she swung the other leg over and vaulted out away from the fence. She fell through space and hit the steep bank sliding, rolling, churning up mud and rocks until she came to rest in a grader ditch full of cold water.

Mud-streaked, soggy, bleeding, bedraggled and half-naked, she walked onto the shoulder of the highway. She stood for a long time, moving from one foot to another, before a truck came up from the south. It looked like a self-contained community, with headlights reflecting on raindrops, diffused by mist, catching the multi-colored lights above the cab. Anne saw a white face peering out of the high window as it passed. Then she heard the bleat of air-brakes, the hiss of escaping pressure, the click of a latch and a shout. As she ran up, the spotlight fixed her in a white conic glare. Blinded, she dropped her eyes and saw herself reflected in the rainstreaked door of the cab: skirt wet and nearly transparent, riding high on broad hips, hair plastered to her neck and shoulders, trailing streaks of muddy water over her breasts. A man's voice bellowed: "Get in, dammit! The other side! What the hell happened to you?"

She ran barefoot around the front of the truck and climbed in the open door.

"Was you in a wreck or what?"

Her teeth clattered as she started shivering. "T-th-there was no wreck."

"Somebody put you out of a car?"

"N-no. I r-ran away. It seemed the best thing."

He switched on a light and studied her for a minute. "You damn near waited too long to run." He put out the light and flicked another switch. A fan whirred. The truck shuddered forward. "Be warm in here in a little bit. Climb up behind there. You'll find a blanket. Get out of them wet clothes if you want. Unless you're modest. You ain't got much to lose, though."

He seemed pleased with himself, and began humming as she undressed in the narrow bunk and draped the prickly wool blanket over her shoulders. She swung out her legs and let them hang over the back of the seat, parting her knees so the warm air could reach her inner thighs. She noticed his hands on the wheel, the thick wrists, the swelling forearms, the tapered ridges of his neck rising up behind his ears. She met his pale eyes in the mirror and smiled.

THREE

ANNE wondered if this was love, what she felt for Hubert. As dawn brushed the landscape ahead of the truck, she lay among the warm bedclothes and watched him sitting high in his cab like the captain of an ocean liner, his broad hands touching the levers, gears, switches and knobs. She remembered how his hands had felt on her legs, on her breasts, on those other parts that she hesitated to name, leaving them blank in her mind. *He put his *** in my ***.* That's the way they would have written it in a book. Actually it had not been that simple, but the pain had been brief, and it was nothing compared to the delicious sensation of fullness inside her. Now it felt like a core of energy in the pit of her stomach, like a wheel of fire blazing inside, turning and touching nothing, seeking more . . . more . . . more. She reached out and put her hand on his shoulder. He frowned as her hand touched him, then seemed to force a smile. "We're getting into Iowa now. Gotta stop and grab some breakfast. You hungry? I'm weak as a kitten." He pulled into a graveled lot full of mud puddles. "You wait here and I'll get you something to put on." He went into the restaurant and brought out a green uniform with white lace trim. She put it on over her nude body and he grinned at her, sliding his hand up under the skirt. She let his hand caress her, liking the feel of it. But when she reached for him he drew away. "No, no. Let's eat now."

She had four eggs, bacon, orange juice, toast and hot chocolate. He was amazed, then sympathetic, believing that she'd starved on the road. While he was having coffee and a cigarette, she found herself looking at the men who came in, her gaze dropping down to their trousers. She desired them, and looking in their eyes, she saw their desire for her. She looked at Hubert. The cigarette had fallen from his fingers and his chin had dropped onto his chest. The waitress came up and said, "Hube, you oughta use one of our beds back there, you're gonna run off the road." He shook his head. "Coming down with something, feel like hell. Maybe . . . . " Standing up with an effort, he paid the bill. "No, gotta make Grand Island by noon."

Anne sat beside him, aware of the sweaty effort he was making to stay on the road. His hands would tighten on the wheel, then go lax. He started shivering. He turned the heater so high she broke into a sweat, but still he shivered. "Guess . . ." he said, "Guess I'll stop when we get across the river. You talk, okay? Keep me awake. Tell me about yourself. What's your name, where'd you grow up, who's the guy who put you out on the road? *You gotta help me!*"

She talked about school, about her teachers, friends, pets. It seemed like another life, another girl. All at once they topped a hill, and the highway seemed to drop away just beyond the windshield. Anne saw the road curving down below like a long gray ski-run, then leveling off toward the river. Hubert was struggling with a knobbed lever; she saw the white line around his mouth, the scared look in his eyes. "Can't . . . seem to shift down. Come over here. Help . . . . "

She slid over, noticing that the dial which he called a speedometer stood at seventy, five points higher than he usually held it. She saw a line of cars coming up from below like little colored bugs winding in and out. She felt a hollow ringing in her ears. It was like sitting in the front seat of a movie theater. A gringing rattle started somewhere beneath the truck. "Push . . . my hand. Push!"

She put her hand over his and felt a shock at its cold clammy weakness. Yet she could tell by the taut cords of his neck that he was putting all his strength into it. *Rattle rattle*. The truck picked up speed as if it were a sled which had just struck an icy spot. Seventy-five.

"Clutch! Push the left knee. Push! Harder!"

She pushed, but there was no way to get leverage, the

wheel obstructed her and so did Hubert. "Brakes!" he gasped. "Hit the right pedal." She found it with her left foot; she was learning fast. Hubert was a sack of meat propped up behind the wheel. She pressed on the pedal, felt it resist her, *hard*. Something shrieked outside the window. The cab rocked from side to side, and there was a grinding, tearing crash. Cracks appeared in the window. She saw a station wagon driving straight toward them, the man behind the wheel staring up, his mouth gaping. The wagon veered off to the right, there was another harsh shriek of tearing metal, a soft jolt inside the cab. Hubert was fighting the wheel: "Can't hold it. We'll jackknife. Leave off the brake. Take the wheel. Help hold her steady. Hold her . . . steady."

She seized the wheel and held it firm. Hubert sank back against the seat breathing hoarsely. The speedometer had frozen at eighty; now it was climbing again. Eighty-five. Ninety. The inside of the cab was laced with little lines like bubble trails in honey. Rock cliffs flashed past in a blur. The truck was gaining on a little red sports car, they were close enough that Anne could see the driver lighting a cigarette. She wondered what would happen when they caught up. They'd all get crumpled up together and roll down the hill like a snowball. But then Hubert sat up and started blasting on the horn. The red car swerved to the right, Hubert pulled the wheel and swung the truck to the left. They were nearly past the red car now, but another was coming up to meet them. Hubert swung the truck back, there was a little grinding bump and the red car slid sideways, flipped over once, and bounced high in the air. Glancing out the side window, Anne saw that the driver was pinned by the wheel with the upper part of his body hanging out of the door; the car was going to land on its top, and the roof would clamp down on him like a huge mousetrap. But she didn't see the event because a cluster of cars loomed up just ahead, three on one side and two on the other. Hubert was blasting his horn but it was no use, all were hemmed in by cliffs with nowhere to go. Hubert closed his eyes and said, "Oh Jesus God have mercy on my soul. . . ."

Anne had no idea how they got through it. The speedometer showed seventy and rubber was burning somewhere. She was holding the wheel with both hands and Hubert was slumped against the door with his eyes out of focus and a bloody drool oozing out of his mouth. On the hill behind her it looked as if a batch of kids' toys had been kicked by a giant, and a cloud of black smoke billowed up from a tanker which had overturned in a ditch. She couldn't remember hitting it. The front wheels were throwing strips of smoking rubber off both sides, the truck was bumping and shuddering and the wheel kept jerking beneath her hands. At last the speedometer showed only forty. Her wrists ached terribly, so instead of following the gentle curve of the highway she let the truck carve its own track, straight across the shoulder and out into the air, ah, it was like flying . . . .

It was dark and her head hurt. She opened her eyes and saw a wall of green corn through the spidery cracks in the windshield. A trickle of warmth ran down her cheek, and she realized she'd hit her head on the roof of the cab. Hubert lay back against the door with his mouth open. She put her ear to his chest and heard no sound of a heartbeat. She remembered her life-saving course and took his wrist. Nothing was happening inside his body. She thought: *He's dead. Whatever made him go, he's gone.* She felt sad, but then she realized there must be several more dead ones up the hill, and soon someone would follow the trail through the cornfield and find her here with him, and they'd take her back to her mother and there would be questions about how she'd grown so big, so soon.

She got a blanket out of the bunk and tried to open the door. It was jammed. She reached under the seat and found a curved steel bar. She smashed the window, knocked out the fragments of glass which stuck up, and crawled out of the cab. She walked down between the corn rows until she came out on the bank of a wide, muddy river. She turned right and walked upstream, beneath the huge brooding maples and birches. When she could walk no longer, she lay down on a pile of leaves and went to sleep.

She felt different when she awoke. She had passed through childhood and adolescence. Now she felt like a woman. She sat up, and saw little tracks in the damp earth around her. The animals had come, had looked at her, and had gone away. Snow White and the Seven Dwarfs. But no dwarfs, no creature with even a semblance of humanity had viewed her while she . . . slept? If that's what it was. The vines around her were wet, the matted leaves beneath her body dry and musty. She lifted her dress and saw that the insects had not shared the hesitation of the higher mammals; with mindless appetite they had bitten and chewed on her body, even now the little woodticks were burrowing into her armpits, invading the curly mat of hair between her thighs. She pulled them out, and the touch of her fingers awakened the memory of Hubert. Even as her stomach growled, she knew what she wanted: First, food. Second, a man.

Desire and hunger were like two rings in her nose; they led her to a spot where the river sent a quiet backwater into the land. She took off her dress and bathed, then finger-combed the tangles out of her hair. She was not frightened, but fully at ease in the middle of nature; the world would take care of her. She pulled the green waitress uniform on over her head, tugged it down over her hips, and felt it settle damply onto her flesh. Then she walked toward the highway.

Three cars passed and the fourth looked like a lost cause too. It was a low, swept-back car painted a bright red; it flashed past in a blur, then with a fishtailing squeal of rubber, bounced onto the shoulder and stopped. She started walking. A man stepped out: young, with dark hair, a long moustache and sideburns. His eyes slid over her face and body. He smiled, but not at *her*—rather at her breasts, her stomach, legs. She felt his eyes still on her as she climbed into the front seat. His hand darted up beneath her skirt and clutched her bare rump. "Well-well-well!" he said.

The man behind the wheel was blond, with bear stubble growing out of a heavy face. He spun the car back onto the highway, let his hand slip off the gearshift and slide up between her legs. It felt good, and she smiled at him. He laughed, and looked past her at his companion. "Wow! What have we got, Irvin?"

As they drove across the long bridge, they passed a bottle and talked about the wreck the day before: Nine people killed, twelve cars demolished, the driver of the runaway truck dead of a heart attack. Anne was glad in a way to learn that all the shouting and screaming had ended, the dead carried off and the wounded treated while she slept.

"What about it?" The darkhaired man was talking to her, his hand squeezing her knee. She hadn't heard the question. "What?"

"Wanta get in the back seat with me?"

"Yes," she said, and smiled.

The two men exchanged looks, and laughed.

The dark-haired man was not as big as Hubert, rather thin and waspy. But that didn't matter. She was vaguely aware that they were passing through a city, but that wasn't important either; she felt her body escaping from her control, sensed her fingers digging into his back, his flesh swelling out between her teeth. There was an explosion against her jaw and he was sitting up holding his neck and looking at the pink smear on his hand. "Jesus Christ, girl!" He looked down at her and softened, touched his lips to hers with a salty flavor of blood. "Sorry, I didn't mean . . . but I had to make you let go. You dig?"

She smiled, because he hadn't left her, and had resumed his delicious movement. She drifted off, and when she looked up again she saw the man with the blond whiskers. There was also a change in the feeling down below, a sensation of greater size and more brutality. After he was gone she lay half asleep, contented as a lizard in the sun, feeling the motion of the car and watching the patterns swirl on the roof. She heard the men talking in whispers, then the car stopped. The dark-haired one leaned over the back of the seat and said: "We're gonna go pick up a bottle. You wait here, we'll come back and pick you up." He didn't look happy. Both of them, in fact, had begun to look like Hubert, sallow and washed-out, with an air of having to push the words out of their mouths.

She started to get out, and the driver said: "Put on your dress first. God damn!" She pulled on her dress and got out. They drove away with a squeal of rubber and didn't look back.

She stood on the corner and waited until the sun climbed past noon. Hunger drove her finally down to the highway, to a sign reading *Eats*. Several trucks idled in the big parking lot, and the smell of the big diesels gave her a sexual stimulus. But the smell of food was an even stronger lure. She walked around back and saw that the kitchen door was open. A man stood with his back to her, scraping the grill, his elbows held high, the black-furred wrists coming down like swan's necks. She thought of how those huge rough-knuckled hands would feel on her body, and a warmth suffused her stomach. But first she had to eat . . . .

When he went out in front, she got a spoon and dipped into a pot of stew which sat on the back of the grill. She had the spoon half-way to her mouth when she looked up and saw him standing in the doorway, his thumbs hooked in his apron. "We generally serve the customers out front, girl."

He was a tall, cadaverous man, with great ears and a nose like a parrot's beak. The eyes were sunk in deep hollows, and there was a wistful sadness in them that she couldn't fathom, that of a man wanting something he could never have. Feeling no fear of him, Anne put the spoon in her mouth and swallowed. "Can I have some more?"

He shook his head. "Not out of the pot. I'll get you a bowl. It's thirty-five cents. Okay?"

She nodded, but her eyes were on his big hairy hands as he got down the bowl and ladled in the stew. He set it on a little table beside the stove. "Crackers?"

"Okay."

She pulled up a stool and started eating. He went out and came back after a couple of minutes. "I looked around. You don't carry a suitcase. And you don't have pockets in that little dress. Bet you don't have money, papers, anything, do you?"

"No." She held out the empty bowl.

He gave her a disgusted look, but filled it again and set it in front of her. "That's seventy cents. You wanted by the cops?"

"No."

He wiped his hands on his apron, a nervous gesture. "Okay. You eat all you want, then you pay it out by helping me in the kitchen. Unless that uniform means you've had waitress experience."

"No. I've never done that."

"Okay." He wiped his hands again and went back to scraping the grill. She ate until her spoon scraped the bottom of the bowl, then pushed it back and belched. Her eyes stung as the taste of onions backed up into her nasal passages. The big hand appeared in front of her, and she stared down at a massive chunk of blackberry pie with a triple scoop of vanilla ice cream. "When you get done there's an apron, and I'll show you how to clean the pots."

Several minutes later, she stood at the sink trying to scrape impacted burnt potatoes out of a baking tin when a harsh feminine voice sounded behind her. "Where the hell did you come from?"

Anne turned, and saw a small blonde wearing one of those high-collared dresses women wear to hide wrinkles. In poor light she'd have been beautiful, for her features were even and regular, and her hair was an almost platinum blonde that lay soft on her shoulders. But in the harsh light Anne saw the wrinkles around her eyes, and the hard glare that people get when they have to strain to see.

"I was hitching a ride with two men. They said they'd come back and get me. But they didn't."

"You mean they dumped you? Where?"

"Over there." Anne walked to the door and pointed toward the overpass.

"Who were they, You get their names?"

"They called each other Irvin and Bill. I waited and waited and then I got hungry. So I came over here . . . . "

"And my old man gave you something to eat, right? Only he's so damn soft he can't trust himself so he makes you work it out." The woman put her hands on her hips and studied Anne for a minute. "Okay. You wanta work we pay a dollar-eighty an hour plus meals and tips. But I want you out front, where the drivers can look at you. You over eighteen?"

"Over . . . oh, yes."

"Oh, *yes*." The woman mocked her, laughing. "You could be seventeen, with that figure, but I doubt it. Doesn't matter though." She slid her arm across Anne's shoulders. "Come on over to the house and I'll fix you up with a uniform. Leave the pot, we've got an old guy who does those when he's sober enough to come to work."

The house was a frame bungalow just off the corner of the graveled lot. A newly laid concrete sidewalk ran between newly planted trees. A few dusty leaves fluttered at the tops of bare limbs. The woman took her into the bathroom and said if she wanted to take a bath she could. The hint was strong that she should as she set out shampoo and soap. "While you're doin' that I'll fix you up with a uniform. My name's Wilma. My old man's name is Ned but everybody calls him Blackie. And you're . . ."

"Anne."

"Anne. . . .?" The woman tilted her head as if waiting for more, then shrugged and walked out. Anne filled the tub, took off her dress, and slipped in. She enjoyed the luxury of warm water and lather. Wilma used an orange-scented soap. The sound of the big trucks pulling out of the lot turned her mind to thoughts of Hubert . . . .

As she was drying Wilma came in with a salmon-colored dress trimmed in brown. She cursed when the dress proved impossibly tight across the bosom and hips. "I do these exercises every day with the woman on TV, have to sweat and strain for what you got naturally. Take it off and I'll let it out." As Wilma plied her sewing machine, Anne sat cross-legged on the daybed in the little back room. Wilma was one who never let the task of her hands interrupt her tongue. "We bought this place a year ago. Year before that Ned and I met at an AA meeting. You know, Alcoholics Anonymous. He was a quart-a-day man, had been for fourteen years. He'd forget what the hell made him decide to drink himself to death, but he was still at it. I was . . . well, never mind what I used to be, I won't name the name. Anyway, we decided we just had these two choices, stay sober or die. So now we work our asses off and don't give ourselves time to think." She passed the seam under the clattering needle, caught the thread between her teeth, and broke it. "You run away, Anne?"

"Yes."

Wilma gave a knowing crook of a smile. "And I guess your folks don't understand you, they gave you a hard time about boys, late nights, not doing the homework, right? Listen, I notice things. You don't talk like somebody who came off a dog-trot farm in the sandhills, or out of one of those crackerbox houses behind the mill. You don't say ain't, you don't cuss, you're used to nice things. Like in the bathroom, you didn't throw on the perfume like it was water. I talked to Ned and he noticed it too. You ate enough for a team of mares, but you held the spoon like so, not like you were gonna stab yourself in the face with it. What does your daddy do?"

"He's an architect. Oh—but he died two weeks ago." Anne had almost forgotten, it seemed so long ago. Suddenly she felt a hot lump in her throat, and her eyes filled with tears.

"Honey, I'm sorry." Wilma ran over and put her hands on Anne's shoulders, looking into her eyes. "I just wanted to get it all out between us, so there wouldn't be any big wall growing up. You got no place to stay, right? So I've got this little room that I use for sewing. This little bed I sometimes nap on in the afternoons, if you don't like it we'll move in another one. You wanta stay with us?"

"Yes."

Wilma's arms went out and drew her in, the way you hug a homeless puppy. In Anne's family such gestures were rare. Kisses were polite and restrained. Touches were restricted to certain areas, under certain conditions. Anne felt the pressure of Wilma's breasts, the warmth of her hands against her back, and sense no limits to the woman's affection. She put her arms around Wilma, and felt the heat between them generate into something else, a fire which had nothing to do with the two of them. Unity of something. We shall, we shall . . . what? Image of the blonde woman lying on the couch at the fort, crying: "Am I part of it? Part of what?" Unity of those who carry the seed, whose function is to hold and save and nourish. Womanhood. And something else Anne couldn't get hold of. She felt Wilma's lips trail across her cheek; they touched hers, lightly at first, then passionately. Anne's hands clutched spasmodically.

Wilma pulled back and looked into her eyes. "You're not—?" She shook her head and clasped her again, but this time her warmth was more remote. "No, you're not, and you don't even know what you're not. So I guess it's up to me to . . . ." She broke off and stood up, stiffly. "I'll get you some underwear and you can put on the uniform. Then we'll go over to the joint and I'll teach you the business."

She learned where the plates were kept, and the silverware, how to make coffee and punch the cash register, how to carry food without getting her thumb in it, how to set the plates down without letting the food slide off in the customer's lap. After a half-dozen dry runs, Wilma and Ned said she could serve the next customer.

Anne watched him drive up in a gray Lincoln. He closed the door, dropped the keys in his pocket, and hitched up his belt—a tall young man made of straight lines: Crease in his pants, jacket falling straight from his shoulders, straight nose, straight line of the mouth, and level gray eyes. He took a table near the window. Anne got the water and a menu and walked out from behind the counter, aware of breasts trembling, hips bouncing. Her body was a well-developed casing surrounding an eleven-year-old brain. He looked up into her eyes as she spread the menu in front of him. She felt his knowledge stab deep inside her, she wanted him and he knew it. She felt her breath quicken and her nipples press against the brassiere Wilma had insisted she wear.

"Bring me a cup of coffee."

She spilled the coffee and felt the scalding fluid on her foot, like a hot iron stabbing through her shoe. Wilma's hand fell on her shoulder and she took the coffee. "You did fine. Now go out back and wash your face in cold water. You're lit up like a traffic light."

Anne touched her wet hands to her face and felt the fire burning inside her, consuming her. She had to have something. Yes. The man. Somehow he could absorb the heat, draw it out of her like a poultice. If he didn't she would simply burn to a cinder.

She stayed in the kitchen until her pulse cooled. When she went out Wilma was adding up grocery tickets by the register. Two drivers drank coffee at the counter while their rig sat outside grumbling in the afternoon heat. The slim young man tossed some change on the table and walked out. He said something as he passed, but Anne's mind didn't register the words. He got into his car and drove onto the highway without looking back.

She watched the gray shape recede into the distance, saw it take the right-hand lane at the interchange, then pause at the stop sign and take a left turn toward town. Not until then did she realize that he'd said, "See you at midnight." He'd spoken softly, hardly moving his lips, yet the words had reached her.

Wilma walked over. "He asked what time you got off, I told him you'd be on 'til ten and you'd be too tired to go out after that." "Oh," said Anne. She felt disappointed.

Wilma saw it and shrugged. "I'm sorry. Don't mean to run your life. Only this guy—" She shook her head. "He stops in once a week. They've got slot machines at the Elks and the Legion Hall and some other places. He's the collector for some outfit back east. Sometimes he's got a girl with him, sometimes not. What he always has is a little gun in a shoulder holster. It's there and it's ready, and he don't have any compunctions about using it." She slapped Anne's shoulder gently. "Just trying to save you some trouble. He's a lot harder than those two guys who dumped you out here."

Yes, he carried death with him. That was the thought which sent her mind back to the underground room, not long ago in time, but in another life altogether. Something remained of the little girl named Anne, because she'd felt fear when she saw the man, sweaty trembling fear which turned her legs to water. But this new thing she'd become saw death and reacted differently, opening herself to it, full of desire, aching to be possessed . . . .

They got busier as the supper hour approached. By eight o'clock she no longer thought about nervousness or sex; men were mouths to feed, orders to write down, plates to carry, coffee to serve, and tips to pick up. The coins in her pockets ceased to jingle, and became a heavy weight which bumped against her hip. Each time she went into the kitchen, Ned had some new gourmet treat for her: Mushrooms stuffed with anchovies, chicken in aspic, artichokes stuffed with crabmeat, beef tongue in cream cheese.

At nine-thirty the crowd cleared, and they were sitting in the kitchen having coffee when the bell rang above the door. Anne said, "I'll get it," and stood up.

Two highway patrolmen clumped in on polished boots, hitched up their guns, and slid onto stools at the counter. Anne felt it again as she served them coffee and pie: the sweaty fear of the underground room, the presence of Evil. She saw tiny dark spots on one man's creased trousers, and knew with absolute certainty that it was blood. *Whose . . . ?*

It was Wilma who got the answer, after a tired attempt at joviality at the cash register: "Just pulled two guys out of an overturned Mercedes." said one. "Ran into a gully about a hundred yards off the road. Must've happened this morning, but nobody saw it."

"Hurt bad?" asked Wilma, hanging up the ticket.

"That's the funny part. The driver didn't have anything but a gash on his scalp—but he was dead. So was his buddy, and we couldn't find any marks on him."

"What were their names?" asked Anne.

One of the patrolmen turned and looked at her from icy blue eyes. "Their ID said Irvin Wilson and Bill Yates. Know 'em?"

Anne felt her mouth go dry. "Oh, I—"

Wilma interrupted. "No, they didn't stop here." She banged down the keys of the cash register and laid out the change. "Funny things happen on the road. You boys come back."

Wilma said nothing more until they'd finished getting things ready for the night shift. As they walked across the graveled lot toward the house, she said: "Now you know why they didn't come back. They didn't act sick or anything?"

"No." Anne frowned, thinking of Hubert. "They were drinking, having a good time."

"Maybe they got hold of some bad liquor. Well, sleep tight. I found some pajamas that'll fit you. See you in the morning."

Anne didn't sleep, nor did she put on the pajamas. She lay on the covers, glancing now and then at the little electric clock on the night table beside her bed. At five minutes to midnight she went out and saw the gray Lincoln parked at the far corner of the lot, near the highway. She walked over and opened the door.

"Wasn't sure you got the message." His teeth flashed in what could have been a smile, but which showed neither friendliness nor humor. He drove a mile down the road and pulled off into a graveled lane. She climbed into the back seat without asking any questions. By now she could make comparisons: In size he was the smallest of the four, but he stayed with her longest. Twice she was brought to a frenzy of thrashing limbs and clutching hands, still he hung on grimly, his breath wheezing in his lungs. Her only complaint finally was that he refused to take off his gun, and the constant banging bruised her ribs. As he let her off he said: "See you again tomorrow."

Wilma was waiting at the door with her arms folded,

hands gripping her elbows. "You went with him anyway, I see. Did you get what you wanted?"

Nodding slightly, Anne started to walk on into the house. Wilma seized her elbow and turned her around. "Well, I can't have that kinda crap going on under my nose. Tomorrow . . . . " She swallowed. "Tomorrow you leave. Understand?"

Anne felt disappointed, but she was too tired to argue. She nodded and walked into her room; her bed had been made, and a little flower-shaded lamp set on the nightstand. Anne took off her dress and put on the nightgown Wilma had laid out for her. As she turned out the light she felt her limbs already weighted by sleep.

She awoke to find the softness of the woman in bed with her, hands stroking her shoulders. "You don't have to go, baby. You stay with me, okay? It's all right, you understand?" Anne mumbled under her breath and slid her forearm across Wilma's stomach, She let her face rest in the soft pocket of warmth between breast and armpit and dropped off to sleep again.

Next day was the beginning of a long weekend, and the restaurant that morning was filled with tired adults and snarling children. Anne got no reaction from the males of this group except wistful looks and a heavy slump of the shoulders, as if their families were riding there, claws dug into their flesh. Anne did nothing but take orders and fill plates. Around one o'clock, when Wilma went over to the house to take her two-hour break, Ned showed her something he used to do in the army: take a freshly baked loaf of bread out of the oven, slice it open at the top, and drop in a half-pound of pure yellow butter. While it is still hot, and the butter not yet all melted, start eating. Add jelly if you like. Anne ate the whole loaf; the butter did strange things to her throat, but she enjoyed it. "More?" asked Ned. She nodded. He said, "You're abnormal, kid. You're a real phenomenon." But he was grinning with pleasure as he tore open another loaf.

That evening they delivered the newspapers; Anne looked through the mesh screen of the dispenser and saw a blurred photo of the man with the Lincoln. Quickly she scanned the words: *Found dead in his motel . . . gun in his hand. Presumed suicide. Underworld figure. Served term for assault at age sixteen, several arrests since then, no convictions*. Wilma, reading the same paper at the cash register, looked up and said: "Looks like you got the kiss of death, baby." Anne tried to understand: The hard thrust of him now limp, flaccid, decaying. She felt sad because he would not be coming back for her. She had to have someone.

He came in toward the end of the supper rush: stocky, dark curly hair, olive skin, bright flashing eyes. Anne felt his eyes on her as she approached him with the glass of water and the menu; her thighs softened, and her breasts began to ache. His thumb scored the edge of the menu. "What I want isn't on the menu." He grinned up at her, his eyes crinkled at the corners. "When do you get off?"

"Ten o'clock," she said.

"Is it okay then? We can sit in the truck and . . . talk."

"Yes," she said, her breath like a sigh.

It was eight-thirty then. He spent a half-hour with his coffee, then walked up to the register to pay his bill. Anne, stacking pie-plates beneath the counter, heard him say in a voice slightly louder than necessary: "Is it okay if I park here tonight? It's that big tandem rig out there, the one that says Crowley Oil Company." Wilma said sure, hanging his ticket on the spoke and dipping into the change drawer in one smooth motion. At nine-thirty, after Anne had bitten her lips until they were sore, Wilma came up and slapped her lightly on the hip. "You make a date with that greaser?" Anne nodded. "Okay, go now before you drop a stack of plates. Lord, I've seen the boy-crazies before, but *this*—!" Anne didn't hear the rest. She was going out through the kitchen, taking off her apron as she went.

She found him lying up in the back of the cab reading a book. The little nook was enclosed by curtains of red velvet. As he scooted over to make room for her he explained that he kept the curtains in his suitcase because the company didn't allow it. "Not that I do this much, you know, take girls into my cab. But it's something I always wanted to do. . . ." Stretching out beside him, Anne let her hand rest upon his hip. He looked at her, his eyes wide. "Shall I . . . turn out the light?"

"Yes," said Anne, her fingers already inside the flap of his trousers.

Wilma was sitting on the bed when she came in an hour later. "What's the matter, baby? Just gotta have it?" Anne nodded gravely, without speaking. Wilma looked at her a long time, then sighed. "Well, okay. But there's some things you better learn. Come into the bathroom." Wilma showed her how to protect herself against disease and to ward off pregnancy. Anne tried to pay attention, but she was so sleepy, and Wilma's ministrations were so soothing. In a daze she felt herself undressed, the nightgown put on, herself put into bed. She heard the roar of the engine as the tanker left. The light went out, and she found herself cradled in Wilma's arms, her nose breathing the soft warmth of Wilma's flesh. "You know you're a strange girl, Anne. You bring out something that I didn't ever figure I had. I don't mean I never . . . in the business you had to please the customers, and some men get turned on by seeing girls do it to each other. I never felt like doing anything on my own. But you know, if it's just lovin' you want, I know ways to satisfy you. I mean of course not tonight but some other time . . . . " As she trailed off into sleep Anne was aware that the hands had dropped to her buttocks, kneading the flesh beneath the nightdress . . . .

Next day during breakfast she heard a conversation between Wilma and a driver at the counter. " . . . had it pretty well cleaned up by the time I passed this morning. Nothin' left but the frame and the rims. You could see where the fire had gone up and melted the guardrail on the overpass." Wilma's eyes slid over to Anne, then back to the driver. "A Crowley oil tanker, you said?" The driver nodded. His heavy cheeks converged into a fat neck creased like the segments of a caterpillar. "Guess the driver went to sleep and smashed into the abutment. Probably never knew what happened."

Anne went outside and walked aimlessly around the back of the lot. She wished she'd never heard about the wreck, never read about the gunman's death, never talked to the two patrolmen. It had been so simple and lovely, to give men happiness and at the same time satisfy the demands of her body. Condemning them to death was another matter . . . .

Still, that afternoon she found herself smiling at the breadman, who was so fat he had dimples over his knuckles. Only Wilma's harsh warning glare kept her from accepting his offer of a ride through the country. That night she tossed and turned until three a.m., when Wilma came in and sat down on her bed. "You remember what I told you? I can take the edge off."

"Yes," said Anne. "Do it."

That night she loved Wilma, but next day she felt tight, jangled and frustrated. Wilma had a tautness around her mouth, and her eyes seemed filmed over, feverish. During the slow late afternoon, while Ned was taking his two-hour break, Anne sat down at the table where Wilma was drinking coffee and said: "I think I'd better leave, Wilma."

Wilma reached out and seized her hands, her eyes were pits of misery. "I won't make it without you, baby. I just won't, that's all."

"But . . . what if it works with you like it did with the men?"

"I don't care. It's got hold of me . . . whatever it is. I can't think when you're not around, sitting at the register I say to myself, 'Wilma, you're a damn fool. You got a successful business and money in the bank and two cars and a husband. . . .' But then you come in and it's all on the scale. Compared to you its a bag of feathers. You're the only one that matters. I'd throw the whole thing in the ditch . . . yes, dammit, Ned too. Just to touch you. I feel like I'm losing my mind."

During the next three days Anne noticed her staring into space for minutes at a time. She giggled often, gave the wrong change, broke glasses. Each night she climbed into Anne's bed as soon as Ned went to sleep. She grew ever more frantic in her desire to please; she wept when Anne seemed cool, kept asking if Anne loved her, if she was satisfied, if she still wanted a man. Anne said no, which was a lie.

On the fourth afternoon, while Ned was taking his break, Wilma took the closed sign and hung it in the door, then locked it. She put her arms around Anne and said: "Baby I don't know what's the matter but I just gotta have you now. I been going crazy thinking about last night . . . . " Anne felt the air on her legs as her skirt was lifted up behind and Wilma dropped to her knees. Then Ned's voice roared from behind: "Well I'll be Goddamned! I saw those people come up and try the door and I couldn't figure . . . . *What the hell's going on here?"*

Wilma broke into hysterical sobbing. She said she didn't know what was the matter with her, she just felt everything sliding away and nothing was important except Anne. Ned put his arms around her and said: "You just go to bed and rest. I'll close up for the rest of the day and we'll try to get this thing straightened out." When Wilma had gone, Anne said: "I think I'd better pack my bag and leave."

But Ned said: "No, don't do that. I've got to go to town for something, when I get back we'll work it out. You stay here while I'm gone, okay?"

Ned came back in half an hour with a paper bag twisted at the top, enclosing the shape of a bottle. Anne waited an hour, then went into her room. She could hear the rise and fall of their voices in their own bedroom. Wilma sobbed a lot at first, then there were shrieks of laughter both from her and Ned. Around dark the sounds dwindled to a low mumble, then faded and blended with the rhythmic creaking of the bed.

During the long silence that followed, Anne fell asleep on her bed. She awoke to see Ned swaying in her doorway with the bottle held by the neck, his eyes unfocussed. He wore only his socks and undershirt. He lifted the bottle and drank, then laughed and stumbled toward her. "She's passed out now, she'll never know . . . . " It had been so long and her hunger was so great, that she couldn't roll away and walk out into the night as she knew she should, but instead turned and opened her arms to him.

Wilma was still asleep next morning, so Anne and Ned opened up the restaurant. Though red-eyed and shaky, Ned seemed gay as he fixed her Eggs Benedict. Anne thought: "Maybe the jinx is finally broken." She went out front to wait on three elderly women who were getting an early start on the day's travel. They ordered tea with exact amounts of lemon, sugar and cream, all different. Anne was getting it ready and Ned was setting coffee cups under the urn when Wilma walked out through the kitchen stark naked, her eyes fixed and bulging. Anne felt a fluttery lightness in her stomach as Wilma took the .38 police special from beneath the cash register and aimed it at Ned. The first shot punctured the coffee urn and the second got him in the hollow of the throat.

He hung for a second while the blood rose from his throat in throbbing spurts, spattering on the floor along with the black stream which reached out from the coffee urn. He took a step toward Wilma then collapsed, bringing down a tray of coffee cups.

In Wilma's eyes Anne saw the trapped frightened look of a rabbit caught in the coils of a python. She turned the gun on herself, but the shot only fluffed the hair above her ear and knocked the top off the gum machine. Splinters of glass and balls of gum ricocheted around the room, and one of the elderly women began to scream. Anne saw an imploring look in Wilma's eyes; she felt an urge to go help her, steady her hand on the gun, or something. But then Wilma smiled and her face settled into a dead calm. She kept looking at Anne while she stuck the gun barrel in her mouth. There was an explosion and Anne saw patches of gray stuff sliding down the inside of the plate glass. One of the older women had fainted beside her table. The other two were running toward the highway waving and screaming. Anne felt a sodden fatigue deep in her bones. She wanted to lie down and let the world spin around without touching her, but a voice inside said, *Get away, get away* . . . .

She didn't remember walking across the lot, but found herself in her room packing the plastic suitcase she'd bought three days before. As she wrapped the little wooden figure and placed it among her clothes, she felt a twinge of grief for the little girl she had been. Life as an ugly preadolescent seemed simple as she looked back on it, and peaceful.

Sirens were approaching as she snapped the latch. She walked out and got into Wilma's Chevy just as the patrol cars pulled in. Wilma had let her drive only once, but she remembered the routine. Her wheels spun as she left the lot; a policeman ran out of the restaurant and waved, but she couldn't stop. She bounced onto the highway and took the turn which led into town. As she drove down the main street, she saw a bus pulling out of the station. She turned the car in to the curb, bounced onto the sidewalk, and stopped. She grabbed her bag and jumped out, waving down the bus. The driver sold her a ticket to Denver, and she found a nice cool seat high up in the back of the bus. The blue light coming through the windows was so restful that she fell asleep almost at once.

FOUR

It was one week after the shooting that David Hall, backtracking on a cold trail, came upon the scene. The deaths of Ned and Wilma Baker had been called murder-suicide by the police. A female employee had fled in the Baker's car, which had been found abandoned in the city.

The desk sergeant explained it to David: "We figured the girl just panicked. It was enough to curl your hair, according to one old lady who saw it. Wilma came outa the kitchen stark naked and shot her old man in the neck; he didn't live to get to the hospital. Neither one of 'em did. I reckon the girl could of told us more if she'd hung around, but we got most of it. They'd all got drunk the night before, and I guess old Ned got to the waitress, and Wilma killed him for it. Kind of a high price to pay for a little honey on your stinger, but I guess we all take risks, don't we?"

The desk sergeant was talking in a nervous rush; David supposed it was the effect of trying to converse with someone who couldn't answer. He clamped his prosthetic left hand on his pad and wrote: *Did anyone see the girl leave town?*

The sergeant squinted at the note and shook his head.

"I guess not, nobody that remembered it. But the car was parked—well, I wouldn't call it parked exactly. Run up on the curb. Right outside the bus sation. So I guess she caught a bus. Nobody's seen her since that day, anyway."

What time did you find the car?

The sergeant looked through a sheaf of yellow forms. "Nine o'clock."

David nodded his thanks, settled his magnesium-alloy crutches under his arms, and pivoted on his good leg. His artificial limb gave a soft popcorn fart as it settled against his stump, and David felt his neck burn with embarrassment. He swung out into the street—half a head shorter than average, with fan-shaped ears and wiry mouse-gray hair which stood up on the back of his head. His nose was thin and his chin vaguely receding; he'd grown a beard in compensation, but the thick glasses he wore for nearsightedness made him look like a bewildered bookkeeper observing his hometown centennial.

The bus station was no more than a ticket cage in one corner of a cafeteria. From the schedule chalked on a blackboard, David saw that a Denver bus went through each morning at seven-forty, while another bus passed at eight-twenty en route to Chicago. David decided she'd more likely have taken the Denver bus, since it had been the first to leave after the shooting. He wrote out a note and presented it to the man behind the cash register. The man pursed his lips, scratched his thinning sandy hair, and walked to a table where two drivers were drinking coffee. After a minute he came back and said: "Harvey Shoop drove the Denver bus that day. He's on afternoons now; be through here around eight if you wanta talk to him. He might remember the girl. All I can say is she din't buy a ticket. Not in here."

David smiled his thanks and started hobbling out. He felt the eyes on him, but they bothered him less each day. Anne had done that for him anyway; he'd almost become a recluse on his parent's old farm, with nothing but his woodcarvings to keep him company.

He climbed in his car and glanced at the clock on the glove compartment. Six hours to wait. He opened the compartment and took out the wooden statuette he'd found washed up on the creek bank. As his fingers traced the curve of breasts and thighs, he closed his eyes and recalled the afternoon he'd lain in the weeds and watched the dragon-flies flit overhead, two by two. He was wishing he'd left behind a wife when he went to Nam, or a sweetheart he'd made it with many times, so there'd be someone to help him over that initial awkwardness of exposing his stump....

Splash-splash. Too loud for a frog, maybe a cow in the shallow part. He raised himself on his good arm and looked toward the water. His heart stopped when he saw the girl. She was tall and skinny, with ribs like a picket fence and a belly button like a wad of gum stuck on a beachball. Must be old Maynard's granddaughter, he decided. She'd just been learning to walk when he left for college. Life goes on, he thought. She stood with her knees touching, and the thinness of her thighs left a two-inch gap where her legs joined her torso. Seeing her little immature cleft, he felt his manhood rise and throb. But he only watched her until she put on her dress and went away.

Her image stayed with him the rest of the afternoon. He found a hickory stump which had been blasted, then burned. The fire-hardened roots were dense and strong, perfect for carving. He whittled her face and figure from memory, but left it rough, planning to finish it next time he saw her.

But the next day she had changed. The pale coins of her nipples had swollen and turned pink. The lines of her rib cage had softened, and her bulging belly had become a rounded, fertile mound. He decided to redo the carving, smooth out the lumpy nose, cut down the teeth that stuck out in front like a chipmunk's. She no longer looked ugly to him.

He built himself a duck-blind nearer the water, and spent the next few days cataloguing distances between armpit and elbow, knee and thigh, studying the dynamics of her hip-movements when she bent at the waist, noting the way her breasts grew into narrow cones and then swelled out into half-globes. He kept saying to himself: *It isn't possible for a little girl to grow into a woman in only a week.* But it was happening. Her brows no longer came down in a glowering scowl, but arched provocatively. The barren hump between her thighs became a glossy red-black triangle. As he hobbled home through the hazelbrush thicket, David wondered if he'd created her in his mind. He touched the bush beside him; it felt real, but the feeling itself could have been a fantasy. He tapped the tough plastic of his artificial leg with the molybdenum-alloy of his prosthetic arm. If he

45

was going to fantasize, why couldn't he make himself six feet four inches tall with shoulders like a barn door and an eight-inch jock and sex appeal that made your hair curl? The answer was . . . he didn't know. That night he took out a block of Brazilian rosewood and started carving, feeling a sense of exaltation as her body came to life in the curl and curve of the grain. Next day he was putting the finishing touches on the statue when she blundered through the tall grass and found him. He looked into her eyes and saw a hunger that matched his own. But he couldn't rise, and he couldn't talk to her, so she went away. That night he composed a letter: *To the bather: I have watched you for several days* . . . . God, that'd convince her she'd fallen into the hands of a pervert. What were the names of Maynard's grandkids? Yes, Anne and Billy. *Dear Anne: Sorry we had to meet under such sudden circumstances. I suppose by the most generous standards I must seem a repulsive physical specimen, but I feel that we are destined to*—He wadded it up with a feeling of self-disgust. Remember, Dave, you're dealing with a unique situation. You've fallen in love with a beautiful woman who only a week ago was a not-too-attractive young girl. So . . . the hell with it. He carved the word *Love* in the base of the two figurines and left them in the little shrine where she hid her food.

Unable to face the task of hobbling down like a crippled beetle, he'd watched next day from the hazelbrush thicket. He'd hoped to see her take a swim, but she'd picked up the statues and gone away. He'd last seen her walking across the pasture, with the wind blowing the skirt up around her thighs and moulding the blouse against her bosom . . . .

David put the statue back in the glove compartment and drove out to the highway. He pulled in where an unlit neon sign spelled *Blackie's* in dull gray letters. One window was covered by plywood sheets, a padlocked chain secured the door, and a cardboard notice was tacked to the paneling: *Closed by Order of the Police.* A heavy somber silence hung over the place, the same as had hung over the pond the day after the storm. She'd left a presence behind which told him: *I am gone. I will not return.* He'd felt it when he viewed Hubert's truck in the cornfield, still unsalvaged two days after the accident: The deeper-than-deep stillness of a graveyard, where the ghosts of murdered men lie in wait for their murderers.

"I heard the shots."

David looked out and saw a skinny boy with coarse brown hair standing up on the back of his head like a rooster's crest. A grin divided his face into two unequal parts.

"I heard the shots," he said again. "I live right over there, across the lot. I saw these two old ladies run out and so I run over and Jee-sus! Blood all over and Wilma didn't have any clothes on . . . . You from around here?"

David shook his head. He pointed to his mouth and shook his head again. The boy's grin faded to an uncertain smile, then changed to a frown when David handed him one of the cards he'd had printed. It showed his name, rank (not specifying that it was no longer valid for anything except computing his monthly disability pension) and explained that an injury had deprived him of speech. While the boy was reading, David took out his pad and wrote, *Did you know Anne, the girl who worked here?*

"Oh, yeah. Only she split."

I'm trying to find her, David wrote. *Tell me about her.*

"Well, she was awful pretty. I didn't notice her shape much, but a lot of guys did. I got this bedroom winda that looks out on the lot. One night I seen her come out and climb in a car with this guy everybody said was a gangster. Didn't wear nothing but a nightie. One other night I seen her climb in the cab of this oil tanker with the driver. He was a Mexican. She was a whoor, my mom said. Mom used to drink coffee with Wilma before Anne came. Wilma said Anne could put a hex on a man." The boy lifted his narrow shoulders and let them drop. "That's all I know. The two guys I saw her with are both dead now."

David handed him a dollar bill, and the boy shoved it in his pants pocket. "Were you in Nam?"

David nodded, and the boy screwed up his face in anguish. "Jeez, what hit you, a mortar?" Dave shook his head. "A mine?" Dave nodded. The boy said Jesus, and Dave drove away. For an instant he was once again riding in a jeep through the scented jungle, en route to take command of his battalion's water-point.

The soundless boom . . . flying . . . a burning numbness

all over his body . . . sensing the smothering waves of pain to come and thinking: *I should just give up.* Next the voice of someone lecturing in a bored monotone, as if he'd already been talking for several minutes: " . . . blew off the left leg just below the knee, mangled his left arm so we had to amputate just below the elbow. The fragment that ripped out his throat missed the vital arteries, fortunately. We patched the trachea so that he breathes normally, but he'll never talk again. The wound in the groin gave him a pretty effective vasectomy—though he's not impotent, just sterile. His left kidney was beyond salvage, and the remaining one is badly damaged—but with the best of luck, no serious illnesses, good diet, plenty of rest, and regular cleansing of the blood through an artificial kidney, he could live another five to eight years. That horseshoe-shaped tubing on his arm is called a shunt. Keeps the artery open—otherwise we'd have to do it surgically each time he's hooked up to the machine. Moving on down the line, here's a 'copter crash victim. Note the X-ray showing crushed vertebra, compound pelvic fracture . . . . "

David went to the office of the Namur *Gazette* and looked through the papers for the week before the murder-suicide. An out-of-town hoodlum had shot himself in his motel. A driver named Luis Martinez had rammed his tank truck into the abutment of an overpass. David added it up in his mind as he walked out. Hubert Reece. Dead. The gunman. The boy in the tanker. Ned and Wilma. Dead, all dead. And here he was, looking for the girl who carried the stinger. Was death what he wanted? He would decide that after he found her . . . .

The bus driver, a thin, blue-jawed man, remembered her. "Bought a ticket to Denver and slept all the way. I remember I had to shake her two or three times to wake her up. Where'd she go? Well I'm not sure. She asked questions like . . . you know, she was looking for some action. I gave her the name of a bar, and she may have gone there or not. I didn't get finished checking in for an hour, and when I finally got to the bar she wasn't there."

Name of the bar?

"Oh, the Seebold Inn. Just a couple blocks south of the bus station. Don't know the name of the street . . . ."

David left at once, stopping at midnight for warm milk

and a cheese sandwich, again at two a.m. for asparagus soup and toast. He napped for a couple of hours at a roadside park, and reached the Seebold Inn at three in the afternoon. The bartender told David he had not been on duty at the time Anne's bus arrived. He pointed to a broad-hipped girl dancing on a tiny spotlighted platform. "She was here then. Grab a table and I'll send her over."

She was a brunette with a sullen pout on her lips. She didn't want to talk, but when David slid a five-dollar bill onto the table, she slumped into a chair and lit a cigarette. "Okay, whaddaya wanta know?" She had the dull cowlike manner of a professional whore, and Dave was glad he'd never given in to the temptation to blunt his body-cravings in that way. He showed her the statuette and wrote out the time and probably circumstances of Anne's appearance.

"I think I know the chick you mean. Sexy?"

Dave nodded.

"Well, you can tell the bitch for me—oh forget it. I was setting with three cadets from the academy when she drifted in like Little Bo Peep looking for her sheep. I never saw anything like these cadets. It was like suddenly I ceased to exist. I got up to do my number and I looked out through the lights and they're all three at her table. One was feeling her legs and another had his hand on her . . . hell, I can't compete against that, anyway they didn't even look in my direction. They split in the middle of my act. Couple hours later some of their buddies came in. They got the name of the hotel from the bartender and took off. Oh . . . the Rialto. A stinking dive . . . ."

The room clerk was sallow and long-haired; Dave rapped on the counter for several minutes before he edged out of a back room and sidled up to the counter. He showed no hesitation about talking, once David had laid a five-bill note on the counter. "Second floor, way at the back of the hall. The room is rented by some air force cay-dets on a weekly basis. Naw, I never saw any girl. For all I know they keep snakes in there. You wanta go up? I'll let you have the key for another fiver."

David felt his scalp draw tight as he opened the door of the room. Smelly, fly-blown food trays were stacked on the dresser and bureau. Empty bottles and glasses covered every flat surface. Mouldy crusts of pizza and hamburger buns littered the worn carpet. It was the bed that raised the hair on his neck. A brown blotch stained the center of the sagging mattress. It stank of dried blood and feces. David dropped to one knee and saw that the blood had soaked through the mattress and formed a pool under the bed. Now it was dried to a flaky hardness. In the bathroom he found towels stiff with dried blood. In the closet he found a short, flimsy nightdress, bloodsoaked and torn in the front where something sharp had been inserted.

He leaned back against the closed door and tried to think. None of the cadets had returned to the room, apparently, for several days. That meant they either knew what foul deed had been committed here, or else—they themselves were victims. The evidence of the bloodsoaked nightgown was clear. Anne had been stabbed. Killed? Perhaps, judging by the position of the wound. Nobody could have shed all this blood and still be alive. His mind felt numbed by shock, beneath it lay grief for the girl he had watched grow into a beautiful woman, only to die before he had done more than touch her hand.

But there was a mystery here. The towels, for example—why would somebody stab her and then try to staunch the wound with towels? Who had carried off the weapon? Where was the body?

David locked the door and went out, leaving the key on the counter. He walked back to the Seebold Inn, took a table, and asked the bartender to let him know if any cadets came in. He sipped his mineral water slowly, regretting that his body was not strong enough to eliminate the poisons of alcohol. He needed that anodyne now.

A few people wandered in, mostly young men and a few women who sat at separate tables, eyeing each other in a speculative manner. Dave's attention was drawn to a young man in a sports shirt, a pair of tan slacks and blue sneakers. He was sure he'd seen him before. The boy took a position at the bar and ordered a drink; their eyes met in the mirror, and David remembered. The same lad had been standing across the street from the hotel when David came out. David lifted his glass and nodded at him. The boy jumped visibly; he slid off the stool and seemed about to start out the door, then abruptly reversed his direction and came to Dave's table.

"You want something?"

His brown eyes were bouncing behind steel-rimmed glasses. He had a small round head, with black hair combed so neatly David could see the blue scalp through the comb marks. David got the feeling that he washed his hands often, but when he looked down he saw that they were grimy, stained yellow between the fingers. Something had happened to upset his habits of personal cleanliness. Acting on impulse, David wrote on his pad: *You know what happened to the girl?*

The boy gave a low moan and sank into a chair. He pressed his trembling fingers to his forehead and peered out through them. "Were you—? How did you know about her?"

Dave wrote: *I've followed her across four states.*

"Are you a cop? Why don't you talk out loud? Is the place bugged, or—?"

He started turning his head from side to side. Dave showed his card, explained that the investigation was a private one, and asked for his help in finding her.

"I don't *want* to find her." The boy's hand shook as he lifted a glass of bourbon to his mouth. "I've been half-crazy. AWOL for five days, I'm washed up at the academy. My girl friend . . . we planned to get married. But now there's no chance. I saw . . . that woman walk right out of the hotel three days ago, after . . . " He stopped to light a cigarette, sucking hungrily on the filtered tube. "Quit smoking when I got accepted in the academy. Quit drinking too. Now—oh Christ! It was a typical weekend pass. A bunch of us always got this one hotel room and took some girls up there and it was always really nice and friendly, I mean the guys would exchange girls . . . . I didn't, because I had plans to get married and I didn't want to get VD or anything. But I always used to go out for food and liquor and stuff, I really enjoyed it, you know. Well I dunno how they happened to meet her. I came in to the Seebold late with Tex and the bartender gave us this message, come up to the room.

"So we got there and Bud and Lou and Mike were sitting around drinking and this girl was eating. She was bare-assed. Mike or somebody said, Take her, we've had all we can handle. And so Tex . . . I'll never forget, she had a pizza, and Tex sat down on the bed and started playing with her. She finished off the pizza and wiped her hands and then took hold of him. I remember thinking, she's a real honest-to-God nymphomaniac. I'd never seen one before. You see, there were six altogether. Seven if you count me. Oh no. I never got into her. I told you I'm engaged to this girl back home. Well then Bob and Vern started puking. They thought they'd got some bad food or something. They decided they better go back to the post and check in at the hospital. That left Bud and Lou and Mike and Tex . . . and me. Bud passed out in the bathroom and I thought he was just drunk. Then Lou and Mike said they felt really lousy too, so they carried Bud between them and went out to catch a bus. Tex was asleep on the floor. He'd had her twice and just couldn't do any more. She's laying there on the bed and no light except the street light outside the window and she said: 'What about you?' "

The boy gulped his drink and looked round-eyed at David. "An' then it came to me that she was an evil witch. You can smile, I never believed in them either. I decided if she came near me I'd kill her, or maybe jump out the window. But she went and woke up Tex. He's the stud of our battalion. But that's all down the drain too. Last week on the firing range a gun blew up in his hand. Bob and Vern never even got back to the post. They hit a semi head-on and I guess there wasn't anything to do but sack up the pieces. Bud and Lou and Mike . . . well, they tried to wake them up when the bus pulled in at the academy but they were all dead. All three. I thought there'd be a helluva stink about that, but there wasn't. Somebody up in Washington must've decided that the enemy had a secret weapon, so they clamped the lid on it in a hurry. But I'm getting ahead of the story. Anyway she got Tex into bed with her. He couldn't see the evil of the woman, to him she was beautiful. But I could see. She was like a slithering reptile, holding the men in her tentacles while she sucked the life out of them. There was this black stuff . . . . Oh God, the blackness. She . . . *it* saw me. And I felt this terrible hatred. That's when I got up and ran." He sipped his drink slowly, then spoke in a quiet tone: "All six died within ten hours. I'm the only one who knew that they'd all been with the same woman. I knew I couldn't convince anyone. I guess I went crazy. I stuck my bayonet down inside my pants and came back to the hotel. This was the evening of the day after; I'd just seen Tex's body, with one hand shattered and the lower jaw blown off. I went into the room and she was lying on the bed, drowsy and heavy, like a boa constrictor after he swallows a rabbit. I said, 'I brought something for your stomach; are you hungry?' She smiled and said yes, and I jerked out the bayonet and stabbed her as hard as I could. The blood bubbled up and her eyes got big and round and she was twisting and bucking. I could tell by the way the hilt was moving that the blade had pinned her to a mattress. She started throwing up blood and gurgling and I couldn't stand it anymore. I ran out of the room and hid across the street in a doorway. I figured she'd start screaming, and somebody would come and haul her away." He swallowed, looked down, and made wet circles on the tabletop with his finger. "She should've died. I know anatomy. The knife went through her stomach, liver and the lower part of her lung. It was a big knife. So how did she get up two days later and walk out of the hotel? I couldn't seem to walk away from the scene, and I couldn't . . . didn't dare go up to her room. Then one morning around dawn I saw her step out on the sidewalk and walk away. She was sort of humped over like she had a tummy-ache, but she wasn't limping or anything."

Which way did she go?

"I dunno, man. All I could do was pray to God she didn't see me . . . ."

Dave felt disappointed. He'd come so close and now the trail was cold again. He had little sympathy for the men who died; they'd looked for an easy lay—and instead had been laid to rest. And *this* miserable little freak had stood across the street for two days, waiting for Anne to die of a stomach wound. David got up, tossed a bill on the table, and swung out of the bar without looking back.

He spent most of a week in Denver trying to pick up her trail. One morning he looked in the mirror and saw that his complexion was turning saffron. He went to the local veteran's hospital, presented his papers, and took his turn on the kidney machine. As he lay half-asleep, watching his blood drawn out and cycled through the filters, he contemplated the state of his one remaining kidney. Eight years the doctor had given him; two of these had gone by already, the remaining six had no doubt been whittled away by assorted stresses and strains. Wouldn't it be nice if Anne could tell him how she did that trick of getting up and walking around, two days after receiving a mortal wound? But first he had to find her, and Denver was a dead end.

Two days later David stood in the barn door while Anne's grandfather forked manure out of the cow-stalls and piled it in a pungent heap. He leaned on his fork and puffed his pipe while David went through the silent, sweaty effort of explaining that he'd traced Anne to Denver and lost her. He said she'd last been seen in good health (with a twelve-inch bayonet wound in the stomach? Well, you had to lie a little) but had left no clues about where she might be going. Now, in order to continue the search, he needed to know what had led up to Anne's departure.

The old man looked at him narrowly. "'Well, I guess you've got your own reasons for wanting to find her. Whatever they are, we appreciate your help. So I'll tell you some things we didn't tell the police." He knocked out his pipe and watched the dottle fall hissing in a puddle of cow-piss. "There was this little girl. Eleven years old. Nothing strange about her except she was so god damn stubborn you thought you had hold of a chain set in concrete. Her daddy had died two days before. Best of health, comes home from a Sunday outing, lays down, dies. Anne wants to stay with us. Her momma's upset, wants to think things out. Sends Billy off to camp. Well, I don't see that, seems like a family ought to come together instead of splitting up, but Norma was kind of spoiled. She's our only kid. So Anne comes down. First thing I see is a faraway look in her eyes. Well, maybe it's grief, so I just watch her. She wanders around in a daze. And eat! My god, you never saw a girl eat like that. She grew too. I don't mean taller or heavier, she stuck out in places she shouldn't. My wife thought she oughta see a specialist. So we called Norma, then told Anne what we planned to do. I guess she took off that night in the middle of the storm. Never figured she'd do all that, or we'd never have mentioned it."

David left, after getting Norma's address. The village was far out in the sub-suburbs, but David could still taste the sooty-metallic smog of the city. He pulled into the drive and looked at the pillared brick home, and the brick walkway winding down to the water. Norma had married well, as Dave's mother used to say.

But she wasn't doing well now. Her eyes were glazed when she answered the door; her robe was wrinkled and redolent of spilled liquor. When he saw she didn't recognize him, he handed her his card and stepped back. A young man stood behind her, looking at Dave with sullen suspicion in his blue eyes.

"Dave Hall. I didn't know. Of course I'd heard about your . . . uh, wounds, but . . . . " She held to the doorjamb to keep from swaying, her mouth loose at the corners. Abruptly she remembered etiquette. "Oh, come into the den. We were just having . . . . this is Ted Chalmers, he was Billy's counsellor at camp and now he's come to tutor Billy in math and science. Drink? Oh you can't. Well, coffee. Not even coffee? Water then. Ted, I'll take another, please. Papa phoned me and said you'd traced Anne as far as Denver. What in the world could she . . . ? And those weird things Papa said about how she could pass for sixteen if she wanted to . . . . "

She was rambling. And Ted's eyes were too darty, too quick. Dave wondered how much of the insurance was left, and how long Ted would stay when it was gone. . seemed too eager to keep Norma's glass filled. David saw little hope of breaking through the alcohol barrier except by shock, so he wrote: *The day he died, did your husband have sexual relations with any woman?*

She crushed the note inside her fist and turned to the young man. "Leave us alone for awhile. Please. You could pick up Billy at school if you like."

Ted left with an over-the-shoulder glare of warning. Norma grew suddenly sober. She sat down on a hassock with her knees together. "I have a right to know why you asked such a question, I think."

David wrote: *I believe Anne is infected by the same thing that caused your husband's death.*

"But—an eleven-year-old child? What can this business of sexual relations—?"

She broke off as Dave wrote another note. *Your daughter has changed beyond belief. It is not possible to think of her as a child. Think of her as a woman with abnormal sexual drives.*

She chewed his lip, then shook her head. "I can't. I mean I don't doubt your word, but I can't think of Anne in any way except . . . the way I remember her. Why are you looking for her, may I ask?"

Afraid she might laugh at the truth, he wrote: *I have six years to live. Possibly the thing which caused her to grow could also cure me.*

"But you said you think it caused my husband's death."

I think there are risks. Death is one of them.

She sputtered with laughter. "A risk! You act as if death is just one of . . . . Oh God!" She put her face in her hands and turned away from him, groping for a tissue. "I'm sorry. It's just that all of a sudden everything got so strange. I mean when John died, and then Anne . . . . " She wiped her eyes, blew her nose, and sat up straight.

"I remember that day very well. One always remembers the last day, I guess. We went to Fort Baggett. Billy killed a lizard in one of the underground rooms, and Anne got hysterical about it—though Billy was always doing things like that. The woman who guided the tour was very attractive, and she made a play for John—my husband. He was no more immune to that than any other man. I didn't fight it—you save your strength for women who want it all and let the one-nighters go by. Not that you don't resent it like poison but—well, anyway, it happened. When we got home John said he felt miserable, but I didn't listen. Later he turned white and his pulse started fluttering. I went to call the doctor but he caught hold of my hand and whispered that the woman at the fort had taken something away from him. He didn't know what it was, but he felt like he was being pulled down into quicksand. Then he said: 'Billy will be all right. Take care of yourself. Look out for Anne.' I always thought he meant, take care of Anne. Just now it occurred to me that he meant . . . beware of Anne. What do you think?"

David wrote: *Doubtful. He couldn't have known she was affected.*

"Affected by what?"

Don't know. Hope to learn something from the woman at the fort.

"Be careful."

David smiled as he stood up with his crutches. Women no longer found him so attractive that he had to be on the defensive. They never had, of course, but once it had been possible for him to entertain the illusion.

He found a chain across the entrance to the fort and a sign reading: *Tour Guide on Duty Sunday's one–five p.m.* David saw an old man with a gold watch chain hung across his leather vest wielding a pushbroom. When David revealed why he'd come, the man grinned and scratched the white stubble on his chin.

"Guess you might look in the state hospital for the insane. That's where the sheriff said he was gonna take her. What for? Well, a month or so ago she tore off her clothes and started running across that field over there. Sheriff had to pull her out of a tree. Kind of pathetic, the way she kept pulling at her skin like it was itchy underwear. Name? Margaret Tuttle. Say, you really handle that claw thing nice. Why couldn't you hook up a screwdriver or a power drill . . . ?"

The state hospital was twenty miles distant. After a couple of hours David began silently cursing the prison of paperwork which society builds around its victims. The administration office told him he should have gone to the Receiving Ward. Receiving had no such individual in their ward. At last a friendly blonde clerk who wore her glasses on a silver chain dug up Margaret's admission note. With studied indifference, she left it lying on her desk where David could read it:

> Tuttle, Margaret. Case No. 21001. This twenty-year-old white unmarried female was admitted for the first time on August 18. Reason for admission at that time was that she thought she had been captured by Indians and was fleeing from them. Sheriff Thayer stated that she'd been afraid of the car and seemed terrified when he drove at high speeds. Staff diagnosis at that time was that of schizophrenic reaction, chronic undifferentiated type. There is complete amnesia concerning her life as Margaret Tuttle. She claims her name is really Nora Gates and she was born in Cleveland, Ohio in 1848. Her fantasy is very complete, including even her manner of speech

and her marked aversion to common mechanical devices, such as typewriters and vacuum cleaners. Recommendation: Patient is placed on Mellaril 100 mg b.i.d.

Visiting hours at the Women's Cottages began at five p.m. David carried his pass across the landscaped grounds and presented it to a large red-haired woman whose biceps swelled out below the short sleeves of her white uniform. She carried it down a long corridor and went through a steel door with a safety-glass window. David peered through the wire mesh and saw a picture of impacted futility. A woman in a shapeless flowered dress sat on a cot; her yellow hair hung in tangles around her drooping shoulders. When she looked up at the red-haired attendant, her jaw hung slack, and her face had the loose pouchiness of one who has at last surrendered. David thought: *Could this be the woman who seduced a brilliant architect under the nose of his wife?*

The attendant came back, swinging her broad hips, and handed him the card. "She won't see you."

David asked if she was definitely the right one, and the attendant sniffed. "Well sure. What do you think, I don't know my own patients? You come back tomorrow if you gotta see her. Or maybe the next day. Margaret has her ups and downs."

She refused to see him the next day or the day after, and the steel door and the formidable protective instincts of the attendant prevented David from imposing himself on her. He took a room in a boardinghouse not far from the hospital and settled down to wait. Each day he visited the periodical reading room of the city library and combed the western papers for news of Anne. He had an idea now of what to look for: Death, sudden and inexplicable, and the presence of a woman with red-black hair and the sexual instincts of a mink.

The weather turned warm, heralding the arrival of Indian summer. The patients were allowed to sit under the huge maple trees, to smoke or stroll on the grass and watch the gray squirrels store up nuts. The red-haired attendant had passed from mere tolerance to active conspiracy; she allowed David to sit on the bench with her, and called the woman over. "Margaret, this is David, the man who keeps coming to see you."

She looked down at her feet, bare inside a pair of unlaced tennis shoes. "My name isn't Margaret. It's Nora." She walked away and sat down under a tree, pulling up grass and scattering the blades.

David caught her looking at him, but when he met her eyes she looked away. He noticed a strange awkwardness about her, as if she were unfamiliar with her own body. She bumped into things, put her feet down too hard. Passing automobiles had a hypnotic affect on her; she followed them with her eyes until they were out of sight. A sonic boom made her fall face down on the grass and cover her head with her hands. All of this would naturally follow, thought David, if the woman had been out of touch for a hundred years.

He wrote on his pad: *The sleeping beauty was awakened by a kiss after one hundred years. What brought you back?* He folded it and handed it to the attendant, who passed it to Margaret, seated on the grass just beyond the bench. A minute later the woman stood before him looking down with a hard challenging gaze.

"Do you know who bewitched me?"

David shook his head.

"Are you under a spell too?"

Again, David shook his head.

"They tell me I am in something called a mental hospital, which is really a madhouse. Is it true?" When David nodded, she went on. "These carriages that people ride in, are they pulled by caged demons who groan and gnash their teeth and give off the stench of hellfire? You do not speak? Truly? Good, then you will not tell me that I am someone named Tuttle and one hundred years have gone in the wink of a cat's eye. God in Heaven, I weary of these words. They burnt the wagon and killed my father and sisters. An old woman took me into her wigwam and kept me there as a slave. She whipped me because I could not understand her heathen tongue. One night I ran away and hid in a cave. I dreamed of a man who married me and kept me in a castle of gold. I woke up in a strange bed, and a girl with big green eyes was staring at me. This body is not mine. I think I died and came back to earth in this form. I feel so empty. My parents, my sisters, my land, everything is gone, there is nothing but these crazy people and a box with pictures that move . . . . "

She started crying, and the attendant put her heavy hand on her shoulder. "It's time to go in now, Margaret."

"My name isn't Margeret."

"Of course it isn't. Come along now, we'll take our medicine and have a nap . . . . "

When David got back to his boardinghouse he found a note from Anne's mother: *Word has come.* Silently cursing the woman's brevity, David drove out. Norma took him into the den and handed him a picture postcard of Camelback Mountain, postmarked Phoenix, Ariz. *Mama, I am all right. Don't try to find me. Anne.*

"It's not her handwriting," said Norma. "I compared it with this."

She held out an English composition entitled, A Day at the Zoo. The writing was cramped and irregular, with tiny circles above the i's. The penmanship of the postcard was a sloping scrawl, without dots or crossings of the t's. David thought it might reflect the muscular difference between a child and a grown woman. The important thing was that Anne had not forgotten her past, as the other woman had done.

He left as soon as he could, promising to keep Norma informed, and drove to the city library. *The Phoenix Republic* reported no mysterious deaths on the day the postcard was mailed—but in Tucson, a businessman had been found dead in his car in a bank's parking lot. It was a flimsy clue, but it gave him a directional fix. A paper from Las Cruces, New Mexico, told of a forty-two-year-old salesman found dead in a motel, no marks on the body, no cause determined, police investigating. It was thin stuff, but it was all he had.

He stopped for cottage cheese and yogurt in Sapulpa, Okla., and had warm milk and whole wheat bread in Shamrock, Texas. Sleep caught him near Tucumcari, N. M. When he woke up he bought a bag of chia seeds and munched them all the way to Lordsburg. There he fueled himself on buttermilk and unsalted crackers, and drove on. The weather was crisp and fresh after the humid heat of Missouri. The motel clerk was bored with his job and seemed to welcome David's inquiry. "They marked him dead of a heart attack. Happens all the time. They get hold of some luscious young gash and they think they're college kids again. You got a personal interest in the guy? Oh, you think you know the girl. Well, tell you the truth, officially there wasn't a girl . . . . " A ten-dollar bill was placed upon the counter and immediately disappeared. "Okay, there was a chick. You want a description, I can't give it to you. All I can say is, wow. She was sure as hell built for the trade. Even while she had this rich dude on her arm, she was hustling me . . . not with the words, but with the eyes. They were green, I think. Hair was dark copper. She was pretty tall, taller than him, and the cops gave his height as five-eleven. But she was built in perfect proportion. I mean . . . oh, food? Yeah, they had some take-out dinners. There's places all along the highway. They deliver right to your bed if you want it. Anyway they had the room ten hours, and they ate five times. I gu ss when he died in the saddle, she split. Or maybe she split before that, I dunno. Nobody saw her leave. Sure, you're welcome."

Three-point fix: Phoenix-Tucson-Las Cruces. The only trouble was the road went in three directions from here. Dave had a supper of warm milk, cottage cheese, and unvinegared lettuce. He bought all the local newspapers he could find and rented a motel room. The papers offered no clues, so he went to sleep and dreamed of a green-eyed woman who offered him a melon-ripe breast and said: "Drink the milk of life." He tasted and found it bitter as bile, so he cried while she rocked him to sleep.

He awoke to the rattle of a news broadcast on his traveling clock-radio: ". . . protective reaction raids in the highlands for the third straight night. And now the local news. The mysterious death of a businessman from San Diego, Grover Maxwell, is being investigated by sheriff's police this morning. Mr. Maxwell was found dead in his camper-truck five miles off Highway Eighty in the desolate Sierra Diablo region some hundred miles southwest of El Paso. A local rancher, Herman Snibble, discovered the body while looking for stray cattle. Mr. Maxwell had been dead for approximately two days . . . . A two-car collision proved fatal to Mrs. William Har—" David shut off the radio, dressed quickly, and left.

He found rancher Snibble repairing a loading chute which one of his steers had tried to kick apart. "Well, I could take you out there, but they already came and got the truck. Rock and shale all around, not even a shod horse would leave tracks. Funny thing was the guy was sitting in the front seat with his pants off. Had them folded up on a hanger in back. Kindy undignified, to die with your pants off . . . ."

David ate sugarless oatmeal in a motel restaurant in Odessa and wondered: Where was she going? The local newspaper gave him a possible answer: In the rugged Davis mountains of West Texas, four sheepherders had died of unknown causes. Alcoholic poisoning was suspected, because the twelve-year-old son of crew chief, Amado Contreras, had survived. *Naturally,* thought David. He contacted the police and learned that the boy was staying now with his grandparents in San Angelo. He drove there and found a shy, slender boy with dark almond eyes. *What did she look like,* David asked, *the woman who visited your camp?* The boy ran into the bedroom and locked the door. The boy's grandfather, a still-wiry man with a sagging white moustache, said: "He is afraid he will die too." David wrote: *I only want to know if a woman visited his father's camp before everyone died.* The old man took the five-dollar note and went into the room. He came back shaking his head. "The answer is 'yes.' He will say no more."

Back in his car, David spent a day crisscrossing the byways of the barren, beautiful countryside. As his eyes searched the roadside, he asked himself: *What would I do if I had this fierce appetite for men—and this unfortunate habit of leaving them dead in bed? Answer: Pick men whose deaths wouldn't be carefully investigated—bums and intinerants, drunks and day laborers, seamen and dope addicts. Operate in a large city, where one more corpse a day would be noticed only by statisticians—and then only months after the fact.*

David drove to San Antonio, where he rented a room and started collecting papers from all over Texas. Sudden death was part of the Texas way of life, but most were explained: traffic accidents, alcohol, drugs, fights, heart attacks, suicides. The ones he looked for were those marked:

Cause of death undetermined. He made one trip to Dallas, where a man was found dead in a stairway. It turned out to be an attempted mugging. He visited Brownsville, where a man was found dead beside an irrigation ditch. By the time he arrived, a suicide note had been found by his wife, and the case was closed.

He bought city maps and stuck pins where bodies turned up. A pattern seemed to be developing in Corpus Christi, but that faded out after three days. In the Houston *Post* David noticed a slight increase in the discovery of derelicts. The pins clumped up in a ten-block area west of the Turning Basin. Most estimates placed the times of death at around noon. David had calculated a man's life expectancy after bedding with Anne as between six and ten hours. That meant she did her prowling between two and six a.m. Possibly she didn't come out in daylight at all.

He packed his car and drove to Houston, where he took a room in a walkup hotel. Since it was only eight in the evening, he lay down on the lumpy mattress and did breathing exercises. He'd read that a good supply of oxygen cleansed the blood and took some strain off the kidneys. At eleven he swung himself out into the glittering street, amid slamming doors, tooting horns, shrilling whistles, and the omnipresent sigh of the freeway. After scanning the faces of a hundred lovely women, he found himself staring at a five-foot photograph outside a discotheque. The breasts which had teased him in his dream were retouched a virulent pink; the face was misted by the artist's airbrush—but he felt sure it was Anne. She wore a tall gold headdress and a pubic covering the size of a coin purse. The sign read:

Princess Maya
3 shows nightly

David entered a square, low-ceiling room with tiny tables jammed around a semi-circular stage. A thin blonde was taking off her panties while a dozen customers watched with bleak disinterest. David squeezed into a chair and ordered a Squirt. A tired comedian came out and told jokes for twenty minutes, followed by a chubby brunette who jerked off her clothes and spent a quarter-hour letting herself be fondled by the patrons at ringside.

The place became fogged with smoke. David turned and saw the bouncers jamming more tables into the back of the room. The bare bosoms of the cocktail waitresses gleamed with sweat as they shouldered their way through solid clots of men. The lights went out and a red spot played on the curtain. The drum beat a sombre rhythm while a voice intoned backstage: "Back in the ancient days before the white man, the Indians of Yucatan used to sacrifice virgins by throwing them into a sacred well. Here on this stage tonight we present the famous death-dance of the virgins, performed by our own fabulous, magnificent . . . Princess Maya!"

Mirrors tinkled in her vaulting gold headdress; silver tassels caressed her ankles from the hem of a long blue robe as she paced barefoot to the front of the stage. She stood frozen for thirty seconds, then, as the spotlight flashed a white stroboscopic glare, she threw her robe wide and held it out like the wings of a bat. The spotlight shifted back to red, the robe closed, and the dance began. David's eyes still burned with the startling vision of her naked body; his pulse pounded as he watched her swirling figure for another glimpse of skin. He was vaguely aware of the waitresses standing with trays tucked under their arms. Anne had involved them all in her own private orgy—first the enticement, then the coquettish resistance, then acceptance. The drum hammered out a hard sexual beat which matched the aggressive thrust of her thighs. She began mauling her breasts—then with a cry she fell to the floor with her limbs spread toward the audience, her cloak limp beneath her. Her hips rose and fell in a dying rhythm until at last she moaned and lay still.

After the thundering rush to the door was over, David wrote a note and signalled the waitress. She took the five dollar bill, then read the note and shook her head: "The princess don't see nobody."

She'll see me. David wrote. *Take her this.*

He held out a paper sack containing the statuette. The waitress took it but didn't move. "Well, look. She's . . . like got a pretty big man interested in her. Better for your health if you look somewhere else. For ten bucks the little brunette could give you a little of her time. Or I could get off for a little while . . . ."

David shook his head. The waitress shrugged and disappeared. Five minutes later Anne edged her way between the tables, belting a black robe around her waist. She stopped a yard away, and looked down at him from her wide green eyes. He noticed that they were uptilted on the corners. She held herself with a calm dignity, back straight and chin lifted. The startling thrust of her bosom and the wide curve of her hips betrayed a sexuality that was more than human. She was a goddess of love. She needed no spotlight; her inner fire leaked out in a faint purple glow which trembled at the edge of her robe.

Suddenly she ceased to be a goddess and became a young girl, wide-eyed with recognition. She folded herself into a chair and leaned toward him with the confidence of one who had known him for years. "Why didn't you speak that day?"

He shook his head and pointed to his throat.

"You could have come after me."

He took her hand and put it on his leg. Her mouth made a sympathetic 'O' and she touched his prosthetic arm with her fingertips.

"And the other parts?" She spoke softly, and David felt a surge of desire. He decided to conceal his capability until he knew more.

He gripped his pad and wrote: *A mine went off beneath me. Sorry.*

To his surprise she smiled with relief. "That's good. It's so lonely with nobody to talk to, nobody I can call a friend. But you know about me already. Maybe you know what's wrong with me. I don't. I've read books on growth and mutation, but nobody ever wrote up a case where you just got so damn big and beautiful you couldn't stand it!" Tears filled her eyes, and David saw an eleven-year-old girl trapped in a big, luscious, lustful body. He wrote: *Do all the men die?*

She studied him for a full minute, her eyes narrowed in speculation. Finally she sighed. "I don't know. For a long time I didn't put it together. The men would be with me . . . then they'd die. I wanted to think it was a coincidence. Then with the air force cadets—you know about them? Well they were so friendly. I wanted to spread out and hug them all at once. It's like when you sit down to a big thanksgiving dinner, you plan to stop eating when you get full, but I just never got enough. Always an empty spot. When the boy came in and stabbed me I thought, It's finally over. But I didn't die. I passed out, I don't remember leaving Denver or anything. The next thing I knew I was in Salt Lake City with just this little bitty scar on my stomach. I was hungry and . . . horny, I guess you'd call it. These harvest workers were going to Idaho to pick hops and I started drinking wine with them and . . . they wanted me. I didn't coax them. I kept saying no but my body said yes. It's like a trained seal that dances for its supper. In the back of the truck we . . . they took turns. When they started getting sick I left them and caught a ride south. For a long time I just went with whoever wanted me, and I tried not to think about what would happen later. Did I ever stay with them while they died? Yes, there was a man who picked me up in New Mexico, he had food in his camper and wanted to spend the night with me under the stars. Around midnight he got cold chills and fever. He started calling me by his wife's name. He held onto me and asked, Do you remember this, do you remember that? His whole life ran in front of him. Finally he squinted up at me and asked, How did you do it? I said I didn't know, but I couldn't help it. He said I should destroy myself for the good of mankind, then he stopped breathing. Everything started going black. I felt like I was coming apart, spreading into a thin net which covered the man and sucked him up inside me. When I woke up the man was still sitting there with his eyes open and his teeth grinning at me. I took some food and walked away into the hills. I decided never to see anyone again. But I got thirsty, and my mind got all warped and wavery, and the rock spires started to look like, you know . . . with their purple knobs and everything. I found a man with long black hair sitting on the back of his pickup watching some sheep. He gave me a drink of water and said, 'You better come back to camp with me.' So they gave me supper and sang songs and I felt so good that I thought: I'm cured. Nothing will happen. They started drinking and one by one they went with me into the brush. All except the boy, who was too young. By morning they were all getting sick, and I left. I don't know that all of them died."

All of them, wrote David.

"Ah," she said. She looked down for a minute. "I dance for the men and it is enough . . . for a while. When I finish work I walk the streets until I find a drunk. I tell myself, they die anyway, of alcohol, or some other thing. And I try to make it pleasant for them, knowing it is their last. But it's terrible, just knowing. Someone I was really in love with, I couldn't possibly do it—but oh, I long for a big healthy man who does not slobber and fall down. I thought it would be wonderful, to be beautiful. But this . . . is Hell. The old man who owns this club, Haverill, pays my rent and buys me gifts so that others can't have me. When he visits me, I tell him I have a disease which is catching. He says he only wants to look, and touch. But I know he wants more, and I have had to promise him—soon. I don't hate him. I don't want him to die. But what can I do?"

David wrote: *The woman from the fort is now in a mental hospital. Claims to be one hundred years old, but remembers nothing. I think she once had the power that you have. Come with me and we'll go see her.*

Anne read the note and shivered. "The thought of seeing her gives me chills. But . . . all right. I have to do one more act, or Haverill will get suspicious. Go to my apartment, it's only a couple of blocks. Grenville apartments, 1004 Bradley." She stood up and put out her hand. He felt the tingling shock as he touched her flesh, then she was gone into the darkness and a key lay in his palm. He got his crutches and hobbled out into the night air.

Hers was a luxury apartment, with rich velvet draperies, jade statuettes, and burning incense. David imagined himself alone with her in this sensual setting. What if he lost his head and blew it all in one final orgasm?

The doorbell chimed. David was puzzled, then remembered that she'd given him her key. He opened the door and saw two bulking shadows, one with an arm upraised. He jerked his head sideways, and the blackjack hit his shoulder like an exploding bomb. He staggered forward, groggy with pain, and felt an upthrust knee drive the breath from his lungs. He wanted to tell them he was a sick man, that a little harmless beating would probably kill him. Pain engulfed him in red-yellow waves, and he felt himself floating down to the floor, soft as a feather mattress.

FIVE

ANNE was always drawn to men who did not desire her. One of these was Bill Ewing, the captain of Haverill's sailing schooner. Stocky and sun-bronzed, the yellow-haired skipper had spoken to her only once, when they were two days out of Galveston. He'd knocked on her locked cabin door and called: "Rough weather ahead. Better take your seasick pills."

Now they were through the Panama canal and sailing into the endless blue Pacific. She recognized his hesitant knock and his high-pitched apologetic tone: "Have to check your beams for dry rot, ma'am. Permission to enter?"

Asking permission was a pretence, of course; she was Haverill's prisoner, and could not leave the cabin unless the guard unlocked the padlock. She muttered an affirmative, lying on her bunk clad only in the bottoms of her red-flowered bikini. The captain entered and began tapping the beams with a little hammer.

"Are you in love with your ship, Captain Billy?"

His eyes avoided her as she stared out the porthole. The seagulls had fallen behind, this was the fifth straight day of blue sky and soft breezes. "I'm not one of these dumb swabbies who think that a ship is a woman. But I know if you neglect her, she'll get even."

"Is that why women are supposed to be a jinx aboard ship?" Anne tugged at the elastic band and let it snap back against her flat stomach. "Because they distract a man?"

The Captain swallowed and resumed his tapping. "She'll

just give a little trouble at first, small leaks, a loose brace or two . . . just to remind you she's there. Then she'll move a hatch-cover out of line so you trip over it, or yaw at the wrong time and stove her bottom on a reef. She's got us in her womb, and we'd better be faithful to her or she'll rip herself open and kick us out into the cold water."

As he walked toward the door, Anne admired the strong wedge of his back, the muscles playing under his cotton shirt. "When's the big night?"

He paused and turned. "I beg your pardon?"

"In the movies, the big deal is always eating at the Captain's table."

His mouth made an 'O'. "Well if Mister Haverill okays it, we'll have dinner together on the afterdeck. The three of us."

Anne clutched her stomach and made a pantomime of vomiting. The Captain shrugged and went out. Anne heard the mumble of the guard, the sliding of the bolt, the click of the padlock. She swung her feet off the bunk and padded barefoot across the springy cork mat, picked up the black, gold-trimmed telephone and punched the button marked *Galley*. "Bari, I'm hungry."

"Yes, ma'am."

She hung up and went to the port. The one-way glass lent a bluish tinge to a distant fleece of clouds. The big black seaman from Curacao, Emil, sang softly as he mended a sail with a curved needle. The muscles in his arms surged and rolled like oiled cables. Anne felt the heat of desire spread through her loins. She tapped on the glass with her fingernail, knowing that he could not see her, but radiating a mental picture of herself lying on the bunk. Emil looked directly at the port, grinned and rolled his eyes, then drew a finger across his throat and shook his head. The message was clear: he had taken note of her desire, but would not put his head in the guillotine. She tapped again, planning to tell him that if the port could be somehow opened at night, the vital contact could be made without the guard's knowledge . . . .

At that moment Notley came along the deck. He stared at the port, his blue eyes burning with savage intensity in his narrow, axe-blade face. His bleached eyebrows came down in a scowl, his thin scarred lips curved in dour disapproval. He turned away and barked at Emil in the incomprehensive English of his native Barbados. Emil rose lazily, teasing the scrawny little man with the magnificence of his body. He loomed a head taller than Notley as the two walked toward the crew's quarters in the stern. They seemed to make a good pair, in the almost-sexual camaraderie of sailors. But Anne knew they were forbidden to speak to her or even to look through the porthole when it was open.

She heard the sliding of the bolt, then three precisely spaced knocks sounded on the door. "Come in, Bari."

The East Indian cook smiled as he wheeled in the serving tray. His white teeth looked almost fluorescent in contrast to his olive skin. With casual grace he uncapped a silver bowl and spooned steaming rice onto her plate, covering it with spiced chicken curry.

"It is only three in the afternoon," he said as she began eating.

"Captain Billy inspected my cabin," said Anne. "It made me hungry."

Bari, still smiling, filled her cup with tea. "The more he feels attracted to you, the more attention he devotes to his ship. When he craves to caress your cheek, he polishes the binnacle."

Anne leaned back as Bari broke open a roll and inserted a pat of butter into the steaming interior. His long fingers were the color of cinnamon, the nails pearl-gray. She looked up into his steady chocolate-colored eyes.

"Captain Ewing loves me, you think?"

"Not only the Captain. You are the spark that sets all of us afire with desire. But since you cannot be touched, we point our energy in other directions. Emil and Notley wrestle in their little cabin; sometimes they make love in the fashion of men. Mister Haverill plots with his lawyers on the radio to make more millions. The idiot guard smokes his ganj and masterbates on the fantail."

"And you?"

Bari took away the empty plate and ladled out cherries swimming in syrup. "I breathe. I meditate on the endless peace of Atman. I contemplate my return to India at the end of this voyage."

"And I eat," said Anne, dipping her spoon into the sour-cream topping.

"Indeed. Yesterday a ten-pound redfish. One gallon of stingray chowder. Four glasses of orange juice mixed with raw eggs in the blender. All the yogurt my poor over-worked bulgars could produce. A pound of dried apricots. Two pounds of assorted nuts. Potatoes, carrots, peas, string beans, rice . . . . "

"The sea air stimulates my appetite."

"I kept a record of the caloric content and consulted a dietician's chart. This was sufficient for five grown men."

Anne shrugged. She would have preferred to avoid the subject, but Bari continued:

"You spend all your time in this cabin. At most, your exercise is limited to pacing on the upper deck when the crew is busy below where they cannot violate you with their eyes. And yet—" His eyes flicked briefly over her legs. She still wore the bikini trunks, covered now by a loosly belted jacket of terry-cloth. "You remain firm of flesh. You absorb a mountain of energy, yet you neither exercise nor create fat. The puzzle intrigues me."

It occurred to Anne that Bari might help her solve the mystery of her body. He was the only man—except for poor David—who seemed capable of regarding her with cool detachment. Without coquetry, she opened her robe.

"And this does not arouse the slightest interest. Am I right?"

"I admire; your body is a wonderful machine. But do I desire linkage? No, I seek to lift my energies to a higher plane."

"How?"

"The average person dissipates the kundalini force throughout his body. . . . excreting, reproducing, eating, thinking. The yogi controls his diet so that nothing goes out as waste. He controls his breath, stops his mind, and withdraws his senses from the body. Thus he attains union with the absolute."

"Will you teach me? Can you?"

"If your desire is strong enough, I can show you the path. But—" He paused as he stacked the dirty dishes. "You must explain to Mister Haverill. Otherwise his thuggee will throw me to the scavenger sharks who follow our ship."

After he'd gone, Anne punched the telephone button for Haverill's cabin. When the old man came on, she made no effort to keep the contempt out of her voice: "The Captain said we could have dinner on deck tonight. I'd like that, if I could sit upwind from you."

"All right, Anne. I've told you a dozen times I regret—"

She put down the receiver, remembering how David had looked when she'd opened the door of her apartment, his face blue as skim milk, his crutches lying beneath him. The plastic tube had been torn from his arm and still leaked a slow ooze of blood onto the carpet. Haverill, waiting in the shadows, had stepped out and said: "It was only supposed to be a warning . . . . " She had leaped at him with fingers curved into claws, only to be struck from behind. She hadn't regained consciousness until the yacht had cleared the Houston ship channel . . . .

As she sat across from Haverill on the upper deck, she wondered how it would feel to snap her wineglass and drive the jagged stem into his throat. Not good, she decided; she had caused the deaths of enough men without trying to bring it about deliberately. Besides, Haverill looked rather distinguished in his white yachting cap and blue jacket, with a silk scarf hiding the turkey-wattles under his chin. The setting sun reddened the scars left by her fingernails, curving down from his cheekbones and disappearing into the gray-blue mat of his beard. A deep tan covered the liver-spots on his receding forehead, and the intense dark eyes made him look much younger than his seventy years. Seeing only his head, Anne could imagine him as a large, powerful man—but she knew the head was attached to a wrinkled, pot-bellied, bandy-legged body at least three sizes smaller than it should have been.

"It's a system of exercise," she explained. "Tones up the body, stimulates the nerves . . . might even put lead in your pencil."

With a scowl, Haverill clipped the end off a cigar. "If you're planning any funny business with that goddam hindu . . . . "

"Bari's a yogi."

"Same thing, ain't it? Go ahead and stare at each other's belly-buttons. But I'll be watching."

The next day she exercised in her bikini, while Bari wore a dhoti of white linen around his loins. The salutation to the sun. Halasana, the plow. Breath control, the rolling of the stomach, Sirshasana, or standing-on-the-head—difficult even in a calm sea. Haverill watched from a deck chair, never taking his cigar more than four inches from his lips. After an hour he went to sit in his swivel chair on the stern, shooting at the flying fish with his Colt .357 magnum.

This set the pattern for the next week. Haverill would watch for the first few minutes, then leave to talk with his lawyers on the ship-to-shore radio, to play rummy with the guard, or to sit in the lounge screening his porno movies from Denmark. Anne felt she was making progress; when she concentrated on her navel something inside her fluttered like a hummingbird.

"The kundalini force," said Bari. "Some day it will burn a track of fire up your spine and explode like a rocket in your brain."

His words made her eager. She wanted to practice all day, but Bari said: "You must not tie the muscles into knots. Now we will learn *pratyahara*. Lie down on the mat, feet slightly apart, hands relaxed, palms up. Breathe the way we have practiced. Inhale for the count of four, hold for sixteen, exhale for eight, pause, then repeat."

She felt impatient with the seam of the bikini cutting into her hips. She peeled it off, then untied the halter which cut into her back. Bari smiled his approval and took up the lotus posture beneath the awning of the deck chair. "Now let your mind flow out into your body. Imagine it like soft putty, flowing, filling up the ends of your toes, fingers, all the spaces of your body . . . . "

She closed her eyes, and still she could see his face, his white teeth shining behind lips the color of eggplant. She experienced a vague perplexity, mingled with admiration. Words appeared on the surface of her mind like shining chalk on a blackboard: *I cannot understand why she exposes her lovely white skin to the sun.*

She lifted her head and looked at him. "Was that yours, Bari?"

"Repeat it."

She did, and he smiled. "Very good. Yes, it was a controlled, projected, directed thought."

"Could I . . . will I be able to pick up un-projected thoughts?"

"Close your eyes and try. Imagine now, the mind expands and fills the body, it goes on spreading like a fog, flowing into the space around it. In the fog you find thoughts like colored balloons. Do it now. Concentrate on the breathing. One . . . two . . . three. After ten breaths you will leave the prison of the body, escape the trap of the senses. Four . . . five. . . ."

She felt the hummingbird flutter in her stomach. It became a second heartbeat which sent surges of energy up her spine. The channel narrowed down to a needle-point of white incandescence which pricked the bubble of her mind, *ahhhhhh* . . . .

She floated in a pearl-gray sea. She sensed little clots and snarls of thought. Some darted about like water bugs. Others floated in the current like egg yolks. She focused her mind on one which looked like a geometric model of straight lines and sharp angles. She saw a pair of blue eyes, a worried taut face. *I'm Billy Ewing, captain of the ship. If you follow the rules, you got nothing to worry about, sailor. First rule is, no broads aboard ship. I read somewhere that seventy per cent* . . . .

Goodbye, Captain Billy. She drifted toward what looked like two serpents intertwined, one black and one white, writhing in mindless ecstasy. One wore Emil's head, the other was—herself. Could this be Emil's vision? She wondered. There was a third presence, a sweaty rat's nest of fear and hate with a pair of tiny blue eyes peering out of it. Notley, the voyeur. Wants to see me make it with Emil. But where is Emil?

Ah, there. It wasn't a vision, but a feeling of life, stretch of muscle, bubble of laughter, the deep booming rhythm of the days cut up into segments which danced in the air like dust motes. *Emil, this is Anne.* Smell of white flesh. She was an odor to him, the spicy tang of lemons . . . .

She moved toward a gray mastodon straining to empty its bowels. Dawson, the guard. Image of a white ape crouching before a cave, showing his teeth. *What are you guarding, Dawson?* Fear roiled up in red clouds, then she saw herself as a tiny figure locked in a block of ice. She was dancing the way she'd done at the club—yet she was not moving, but was frozen at the instant where she threw open her robe. At the point of her pubic beard two pink lips held one of Haverill's giant cigars. She saw the old man's gray dentures clamped around it. Haverill was gunmetal, bite of steel whips, fishhooks of pain. To Dawson, Haverill was fear. To Haverill himself . . . .

Running on a treadmill. Faster, faster. Jesus it's catching up with me. Body decaying. Teeth gone. Stomach fucked up. Balls going, going fast. If I could get it up just once more. What's wrong? It worked okay before she showed up. Castrated me with her eyes, the supercilious bitch. I'll make it with her once and then I'll kill her. I'll kill her anyway, that's just as good, the look in their eyes when they die, no different than popping your nuts, dying is just the big come and life's a jackoff from start to finish . . . .

Anne felt herself leaving the ship, floating high in the air. She saw the sea far below, in razor-sharp detail, as if viewed through the wrong end of a telescope. *I'm a bird.* She wriggled, propelling herself through liquid. *I'm a fish, oh what fun this is . . . .*

After a long time she became aware of a loving but insistent presence which brought her back to her body. She felt the pressure of the mat against her back. She sighed and wriggled her fingers; they crackled with static electricity . . . .

She opened her eyes and looked at Bari. "I found everybody but you."

"One cannot see his shadow when radiance is everywhere. Our minds were one."

She felt a tingle of warning. "Then you know all about me."

He nodded, slowly. "But there are mysteries. You are a young girl, and yet you have the body of a woman."

"Is that unusual?"

"No. But there is an area I cannot penetrate." He frowned, and his eyes seemed to lose focus. "Above the neck. To the right of the *agña cakram.* A dormant force which doesn't fit the rest of you. Your life energy flows around it, does not enter."

She had an image of the gelatin blob on the wall of the underground room. "Is it . . . some kind of parasite?"

"Perhaps. Concentrate inside your skull, just behind the right ear. Tell me if you feel any sensation in that area."

Anne closed her eyes. The shrill ringing in her ear descended to a mellow note, like the hollow sound of a gong. She felt lightness pervade her body, as if it were about to break contact with the mat and float upward. *Hello,* said a voice inside her mind. *I found it. Now I'm going in.*

Silence. Itching deep inside her right ear. Bzzzz. Bzzzz. Hot shards of pain like sparks from a grindstone. A verbalized thought: *Worms in hot ashes.* And then . . . something else.

It was so far beyond her experience that her mind could not contain it. The thread of consciousness was cut and joined together again. She lay trembling and rigid, recalling an explosion of sound, like a sheet of iron dropped from a great height, then the echoes whang-whang-whanging through the cavern of her skull.

Bari, Bari, what happened?

His answer came from far away. *You heard. It screamed.*

Anne felt a sense of grasping, seizing, possession. She opened her eyes to see Haverill step onto the deck. "What the hell's going on up here?"

"We're phasing our minds," said Anne.

He glared down at her body, working his lips as though he were about to spit. Then he took off his robe and threw it over her hips. "Bari, get me a gin and tonic." When Bari had gone, Haverill growled: "Don't lay around bare-assed. Gives 'em ideas."

"Not Bari. He's not on the physical trip."

"Moves like a snake," said Haverill, ripping off the end of a cigar with his teeth. "I don't want the sonofabitch around. I'm gonna have him put off."

It gave her a fluttery, lost feeling—the prospect of losing the only friend she'd found, besides David. She sat up and tried to keep her voice calm as she explained: "I don't care for Bari as a person. It's just that he knows about things other people don't even think about, and I think he can help me . . . . "

She stopped as Bari came on deck, unfolded a three-legged serving tray, and placed a frosted glass in its exact center. With a slight bow and a catlike flick of his eyes in Anne's direction, he backed to the ladder and went down.

Anne jumped as a hot flash of pain shot through her leg. Haverill had caught a soft chuck of her inner thigh between knuckles of his first two fingers and twisted. He spoke through his clenched teeth: "Don't care for him as a person, eh? Think I'm a senile old jackass, don't you?" His eyes slanted with hate. His grip was surprisingly strong for an old man.

In a sudden savage reaction, her hand lashed out, so quickly she saw only the blur of her curved fingers raking across his face. Three red streaks appeared below his right eye, with ruby droplets of blood welling up. Haverill fell back, holding his hand to his cheek. "Dawson! Get up here!"

Anne ran from the stairway but the man-mountain had already started up. She kicked out with her foot, felt the instep smash the soft parts of his genitals—but Dawson had the implacable momentum of a charging grizzly. Even as his face twisted from the pain of her blow, he pinned her arms in a bear hug and squeezed until her vertebra popped inside her like a string of buttons. She gasped for breath as her rib-cage pressed in on her lungs. Dimly she heard Haverill telling Dawson to lock her in her cabin. She felt herself being carried down the gangway with Dawson's knee thumping into her bare rump with every step. She saw Captain Ewing staring out of the pilot-house, his face frozen in shock. Emil stood on the deck below grinning like a great joyous idiot. Notley pretended to be coiling a rope, peering avidly from the corner of his eyes . . . .

Lying on the floor of her cabin she heard the Captain raise his voice: " . . . don't give a god-damn if you are the owner. There'll be no beating of women on my ship."

Haverill said something inaudible, then the Captain replied in a tone that was softer, but weighted with exasperation: "Mr. Haverill, the nearest landing is the Marquesas, seven hundred miles southeast of here. That's over a week of tacking into the wind. It's not worth it, just to put one man ashore."

She heard part of Haverill's incoherent reply, then both voices receded. Examining herself, Anne found red spots

slightly nearer than the Marquesas. Now they were heading into the prevailing winds, and Bari was spending the night shut up in the paint locker to meditate on his sins. "An' I got the key," said Dawson.

When she let him out, Anne said: "Later tonight. All right?" The brute nodded once, then frowned uncertainly.

Around ten he tapped on her door. When she let him in he held his stomach and said: "I don't really feel up to it. This damn ship's bouncing around like a roller-coaster."

"Lie down on the bunk."

"But Haverill—"

"He won't come around. Don't you imagine he's sick too?"

Within minutes he was snoring on the bunk. Anne took the key from his pocket and prowled barefoot on the deck. The wind howled, the gibbous moon shed a cold light on the white-toothed sea. High amidships, she saw the silhouettes of Emil and Notley as they fought to secure a flapping sail.

She opened the paint locker and slipped inside. By the dim red light of a ten-watt bulb, she saw Bari sitting calmly with pieces of short rope on the deck beside him. "The knots were simple," he said. "I was just about to undertake the lock."

Dark bruises marked his face, one eye was closed, his nose had swollen to a bulbous lump. She knelt beside him and touched his forehead, but he smiled. "My mind does not feel the pain. Only the body reacts."

"You know they're going to put you off at Malden Island?"

"No. That will not be. I cast my mind into the future and I see something else."

"What?"

He shook his head. "If I told you, then the future would be introduced to the present. All would change."

"Well, why not, if the future is bad?"

"It is . . . nothing. I am nothing. You are the mover. What is happening inside your head?"

She let her mind become inactive the way he had taught her; it was like holding a washbasin full of water until it ceased to ripple. "There's a spreading numbness behind my right ear, like when the dentist deadens your gums with novocaine."

Bari nodded. "I pick up its thought, or what passes for thought. Infantile rage. I disturbed it, now it wants to kill me." He paused and took a deep breath. "I do not know if it is intelligent or not, but somehow it influences those around you. I feel the hatred of everyone on board, they think they are acting logically, but they are being used by the creature to destroy me."

"We'll take the dinghy and get away. Can you handle it?"

"Yes." He smiled, but his eyes were sad. "All right. Let it be done that way."

They found the boat on its divots and lowered it to the water. It bounced like a cork on the turbulent sea. Bari stepped into the stern and reached up to take her hand. As their flesh touched, she realized why he had smiled. "If the thing is in me . . . then it will go on trying to kill you."

"Yes."

"You'll have to go alone then."

"I know. Goodbye, Anne."

He was only yards away when she felt a crushing weight of despair. "What can I do, Bari? How can I get rid of this thing?"

"Try to put love in its place."

She watched him ship the oars and tug on the cord which started the outboard motor in the stern. As the exhaust sputted, she remembered the most important question: "What is love, Bari?"

She thought at first that the outboard motor had backfired. But then Bari fell away from the stern as though smashed by a giant backhanded blow. He fell across the thwart, and a dark fountain erupted from his chest. His blood looked like ink in the moonlight. Anne turned and saw Haverill standing at the railing, above and behind her. His pajamas were wrinkled and drawn up around his narrow calves. The gun in his hand bucked and spat a tongue of flame over her head. She turned back and saw the little dinghy turn crossways in the waves, saw the dark shape of Bari rise and stand swaying in the boat. He held both hands to the spouting hole in his chest, and Anne saw that another had appeared in his side, just above the hip. She had once seen him drive a curved sailor's needle through his hand without drawing blood, but she didn't think his flesh could stand against a magnum slug. Two more shots crashed overhead. Bari's head jerked, and he gave a little springing leap sideways out of the boat. For a second she could see his dark shape awash in the sea, then it sank. Anne closed her eyes. Bari's face filled her brain. His smile was brilliant as the sun. *Love is surrender* . . . .

She heard the grunting of males in combat. Looking up, she saw that the shadow of Haverill had been joined by the bulky silhouette of Captain Ewing. The pistol crashed again, this time sending the fire upward. The Captain seized Haverill's wrist and forced it back; he wrenched the gun easily from the old man's hand. Haverill charged, but Ewing sent him sprawling backward with a shove. The old man lit yelling: "Dawson! Dawson, get up here!"

The Captain's voice was taut but calm. "You won't need your trained gorilla. The gun was all I wanted."

"Ewing, you've had it. You're fired."

"You may relieve me of command when we reach port. Meantime I'm charging you with the murder of my cook."

"You can't make it stick. He was stealing a boat—"

"Shut up. Emil! Get the dinghy."

The big black man stepped to the rail, swung a grappling hook, and threw it like a lasso. Haverill stomped away, barking for Dawson. With no clear idea in her mind Anne followed him. Over his shoulder she could see Dawson lying on her bunk, eyes closed, apparently asleep. Haverill rushed to the bunk and seized him by his lapels. "Dawson, you stupid ass—!"

Dawson's head rolled. A sudden lurch of the ship spilled Dawson onto the deck with the sodden thump of a filled sandbag. One of his hands flopped at Anne's feet, and she saw a flower tatooed on the fleshy part of his hand between thumb and forefinger. Beneath it was the word *Love.* Could be listed as the cause of death, thought Anne. She was vaguely aware that her mind was still numbed by the shock of Bari's death.

"Overdose of drugs," said the Captain behind her.

"Bullshit," said Haverill. "You don't overdose on weed, and Dawson didn't use hard stuff." He bent over the body, his back hiding it from Anne's view. "Must've been something he ate. Your damn cook poisoned him, I suspect, on your orders. Had to get him out of the way, before you could get me."

"Don't be a damn fool, Haverill. You're in a poor position to make accusations."

"Am I?" The old man whirled around, pointing a snub-nosed revolver with shaking hand. "Does this look like a poor position? Eh?" He cackled. "Didn't think about Dawson carrying a piece too, did you? Damn fool, am I? That's what you are, Ewing. Now put your hands above your head and don't move. Anne, take my gun out of his pocket and bring it to me."

Anne felt as though her body had turned to lead. She could not accept the reality of the two men who faced each other over the body of the fallen Dawson. They seemed like models made of air-filled plastic; they would shoot at each other with their toy guns, and one would appear to die. The survivor would claim her body as his prize and they would copulate with the dry rasping squeak of styrofoam . . . .

"Anne, what's the matter with you?" Haverill's eyes darted in her direction, then shifted quickly back to Ewing.

"I'm tired." At that moment fatigue hit her, like an anvil laid on her shoulders. "You're not in danger. You'll never be punished for killing Bari. So the hell with it. I'm going to lie down in somebody else's cabin."

She turned and started out. Behind her, Ewing said: "I'm leaving too, Haverill."

"Ewing! I'll shoot!"

The Captain paused in the doorway and turned. "I don't think you've lost your mind completely. How could you get to port, if I were dead?" He stepped outside and started to close the door. "When you get tired of sharing the cabin with a dead man—and believe me the smell rises fast in the tropics—then you can throw your gun out the door and I'll take care of the body."

Haverill stood holding the gun, a look of wide-eyed bewilderment on his face. Anne had never seen him this way, so obviously a befuddled, confused old man. Or could it be that the . . . *It* that she carried had taken control of his actions? If so, then Captain Ewing was making a mistake, standing there so calmly sliding the bolt . . . .

Inside the gun barked three times. Three splintered holes

popped out in the teakwood door, each a foot higher than the other, slanting up toward the right. The Captain spun around with a look of surprise on his face, stumbled once, and fell forward. His fingers clawed the planking as he tried to rise. He managed to lift his head a couple of inches before his strength gave out. His chin thunked on the deck. His legs slowly straightened to a trembling rigidity; he passed wind with a loud raucous blatt, then went limp.

Anne felt faint. Her lips hurt from being bitten, her skin prickled as though it were just regaining sensation after being numb for several hours. She watched Haverill come out of the cabin holding the gun at his side. He looked like a rodent emerging from its hole. Even his nose seemed to twitch. He was breathing in short gasps, holding his left hand against his sternum.

"Told him . . . he was a damn fool. Didn't think . . . I could learn to sail this ship. Hell. Learned to fly a plane in two hours. He's got books . . . charts in his cabin . . . ."

Anne saw a movement in the sea. "Who's going to handle the sails, Captain Haverill?"

"The crew, of course. What the hell are you smiling at?"

He whirled to follow her gaze. The schooner sank into the hollow of a swell, wallowed for an instant, then soared up again. The little dinghy rode another crest, at least a hundred yards distant. Against the shining water Anne saw the bulk of Emil pulling the oars, while Notley sat in the bow like a coxswain.

Haverill ran to the rail. "You men! Come back! I'll pay you a hundred dollars a day!"

The dinghy dropped out of sight. The yacht nosed down, shook itself like a wet dog, and struggled up. The dinghy had receded another twenty yards distant. Emil was pulling the oars with a rapid, piston-like beat. Haverill bellowed:

"Two hundred dollars a day!"

Emil rowed faster. Anne laughed. "They think you're a homicidal nut, Haverill."

"Shut up. Five hundred dollars, men! Five—"

He broke off as the boat slid sideways into a trough, and the sea poured over the side. For a moment Anne stood in knee-deep water, then the boat rose up again. Haverill stared down at the water rushing over his feet. "A thousand!"

"I'm going to lie down, Haverill."

"Wait. Ahoy, the dinghy! One thousand dollars. One thous—" He broke off with a look of astonishment on his face. He turned his head toward her, started to speak, then collapsed on the deck. "My . . . pills. In my cabin. Please!"

She went in, found the tiny canister of tablets which he usually wore clipped to his shirt pocket, and went back. He was holding the rope in a death-grip, and water was streaming off his body. She pushed a tablet between his lips and felt him swallow. After a minute his breathing slowed to normal.

"Insanity," he said a long time later, lying propped up in his bunk. "Something just came in and kicked me out of the driver's seat and took the wheel. I'm not a nice man, never pretended to be. But I'm not stupid either. Things I was doing, I kept thinking: You dumb bastard, there's no profit in this. But I did them all the same . . . . "

He trailed off and closed his eyes, breathing softly as if in sleep. She got up and went out of the cabin. He was dying, they both knew that, the question was whether he would go down before the ship did. Morning had come, but no sunshine. The clouds boiled low over the ship, the rain slanted down in sheets. The deck was littered with seaweed and foam, something had broken loose and crashed through the railing on the other side but she couldn't tell what it was. A sail whip-cracked overhead, showering her with moisture. She thought she should secure it somehow before it tore itself apart, but she had no idea where to tie the loose end. As she looked up into a tangled mess of snarled lines and flapping canvas she knew she was incapable of making even the slightest improvement in their condition . . . .

Hearing Haverill moan, she went back in. His eyes were the only thing left alive in his face. They glittered darkly in a death-mask as he moved his lips.

"You did it," he said finally. "You let something loose, you and that hindu, when you started poking around inside your mind. I knew the minute it happened. Like a dark filter coming between me and the light. All my friends became enemies . . . . " He closed his eyes and breathed with his mouth open. "I've been afraid all my life. Back home in Goose Creek I was always the little guy. I had rickets when

I was a kid, my head grew and the rest of me didn't. I got into boxing when I was twelve. Trained up to the district golden gloves, featherweight class. I didn't have much power, but I kept working my fist in his face like a jack hammer. This Mexican kid from Harlingen, I peeled him like hamburger. Nobody messed with me. My mom scrubbed floors and did people's washing to get me through high school. They used to tell us poor folks, get a high school diploma and earn big money. By the time I got one they'd raised the bar another notch. So I went to Texas A & M. Started supplying booze to frat houses. This was back in the bad old prohibition days. I took on some muscle-boys to keep the hoods from taking over my business. Third-string athletes, mostly. My business got so big I had to drop college. But I had a car. A house. And—for the first time in my life—girls. All the girls I wanted. I gave the little darlings anything they asked for. When prohibition ended I went into night clubs. Some of the college girls wanted to make expenses hustling drinks. When I found out most of them were whoring on the side, I just took over their arrangements. Must've had fifty whorehouses during the thirties. Politicians and cops got in free. I started getting good tips on war contracts, went into oil and chemicals. I'm worth fifty million on paper . . . support all the red white and blue causes . . . guess I've had a full life . . . never had time to worry about being happy. There was always something to get, then when you had it, you saw something else." He opened his eyes with an effort. "Moneybelt around my waist . . . about ten thousand cash. Yours. Locket on a gold chain . . . can you get it out for me?"

She opened the flap and took out the locket. There was a miniature photo of a gaunt, tired woman with hair pulled back behind her ears. "Your mother?"

"No . . . just a picture. Window dressing. Press on the face of it, turn counter-clockwise. Key inside. See it? Okay, close it up. Put it around your neck. If you make it back to Houston, go to the Texas Chemical Bank, safe deposit box four-three-five. Show the locket to the president, if they give you trouble. There's jewelry . . . cash. Half a million dollars' worth. Yours . . . if you do one more thing for me." His hand came out and touched her knee, crept slowly upward like an ancient spider.

Anne felt like laughing, his intent was so ludicrous. "That's what killed Dawson. And a lot of other men you don't know."

His wrinkled old lips leaked a snail's track of drool into his beard. "Don't care . . . dying anyway." A froth of pink bubbles appeared on his lips. "Can't move. Getting dark. Anne . . . dance for me. Please."

She danced—not with the headdress and the long blue cape, but with a silk coverlet she pulled off the old man's bed. The only rhythm was the drumbeat in her mind, the only sound was the slap of her bare feet on the deck. As she threw off her covering and danced naked, the old man's breathing gew hoarse and ragged. She loved him for a moment. He was . . . her father, her grandfather, the school principle, the President of the United States, all the figures of male authority she'd been conditioned since birth to obey. And because he was the only male within miles of blue water, he came to represent . . . Man. Even after his breathing ended, and the sightless eyes had sunk back into their sockets, she felt regret that her dance had not awakened one last final spark of life. She looked at the limp and wrinkled vestige of his manhood, sighed, and walked out on deck.

She felt washed out, bitter and alone. The wind had stopped, the sea rose and fell in oily swells. The body of Ewing lay face up, the legs wedged under a cargo hatch. His head rolled from side to side with the motion of the vessel; the creak of timbers became his voice saying: "No . . . no . . . " A seagull with a yellow beak landed on the Captain's chest, fluffed up his wings, and pecked out his eye. The bird turned to look at her, blinked, and swallowed. "Want some?"

Anne jumped at the gull and waved her hands. "Shoo!" The bird flapped away and lit on a railing only a few feet away. Should throw the body overboard, she thought. She looked at the calm sea and remembered a movie where the body of a murdered man had floated around the ship. *Have to wrap him up and weight him so he'll sink.* She went into her stateroom for a blanket and saw the body of Dawson. She took hold of his leg and tried to drag him outside, but his joints had stiffened. A cloud of flies rose up, then settled again on the corpse. A ripe odor of decay filled the room. *Here am I in the presence of death.* She ripped down the shower curtain and managed to wrap Ewing in it. She felt unusually weak, and had to pause for breath after she finished. She went into Haverill's cabin and wrapped the old man in a blanket. He felt surprisingly light as she carried him out on deck; she thought his bones must be hollow, like a bird's. But then as she moved Dawson, she realized she was gaining strength. *Catching my second wind,* she decided. Still she didn't feel really good. She looked at the three bodies laid out on deck, and thought of weighting them and throwing them overboard. *Easier to jump overboard myself.* Crazy thought. The world trembled and slid sideways. She opened her eyes and saw the deck only an inch from her eyes. Her nose stung with residual pain. Must've bumped it when I fell. Terrible feeling, to faint. Like getting hit with a hammer. She hadn't recovered yet, in fact. Reality was a thin-woven fabric stretched over a pit of blackness. She didn't want to look into the blackness. The thing that Bari had awakened was hiding in there, watching her with little red eyes. She wouldn't look, it was Evil. Bari had tried to make her look at it, that was the reason she had—

I didn't kill him!

You set it up so Haverill would have an excuse to kill him. You fed his jealousy.

That wasn't me. That was . . . .

Something you contain? Ha. If you contain it, it's you.

Shut up.

The voice fell silent, but her head began to throb. She decided to rest before dumping the bodies. Her own cabin stank of death, so did Haverill's. She went to the Captain's quarters and stretched out on a bunk, looking at a framed photograph which hung on the wall. A pretty brown-haired woman stood on a sloping lawn in front of a red-tiled stucco house. She held an infant in her arms and rested her hand on the shoulder of a boy. He looked about three years old. Jeri, Joanie and Timmy were their names. She couldn't recall that Ewing had ever told her he was married. Oh well. She closed her eyes. *Timmy needs me. Mothers are too damn permissive. Jeri . . . wonder if she's hitting the pills again. She said she didn't mind me taking this long charter. That's not normal, is it?*

Anne opened her eyes with a start. The voice in her mind had been Captain Ewing's. Was it possible that by lying on his bunk, she could pick up his thoughts?

She closed her eyes again. She could see a lumpy cigarette rolled in brown wheat paper. She smelled the hot pungent smoke, felt the sweet relaxation. *Now,* she thought, *I am Dawson.* Haverill was there too. She saw the inside of a safe deposit box. Stacks of stock certificates. Metal boxes with jewels inside, money. Cash, cash, lots of cash . . . .

Enough of Haverill. A vast herd of sheep drifted like smoke over the hillside, their hooves clicking on the rocks. Hot bite of tequila going down, a thought in Spanish: *Querida mia.* Image of a girl with a flower in her hair, dress whirling around her legs. That was the sheepherder, she thought.

She let her mind sink further into the blackness. Clacking, quacking voices . . . everybody thinking at once. *Hope I get a three-day-pass this weekend . . . . That dirty son-of a-bitch! Cut around me and damn near tore my bumper off . . . . Gotta reach Grand Island by noon . . . . I thought you loved me Clara, I didn't know about the baby . . . . No indeed sir. If I am disbarred, the legal profession will lose a sincere, devoted, servant . . . . Thirty thousand shares of Anaconda bought on margin . . . .*

A familiar picture flashed before her eyes: the little truck-stop cafe, the row of plastic-padded stools, the cake display case. Naked woman with a gun. My God it's Wilma. Shock of hammerblow in the throat. Oh the cruel pain. *I was drunk, Wilma. I didn't think. I never had a strong will, you know that . . . .*

Ah God. She couldn't sleep. All those people who had died, their memories, their dying thoughts, she contained them. *I am a graveyard.* That's what lies in the darkness that Bari couldn't enter. Only they aren't dead. They're alive, locked up inside that little cyst of blackness.

Seal it off. You can't live with it, Anne. Forget it. Go to sleep.

She closed her eyes. *No, she and the kids will make out. There's fifteen thousand insurance . . . Can't understand it.*

Had my doctor's checkup two weeks ago . . . If I write an order for four thousand, say, I'll stop by and get one of those slick cunts in Vegas . . . .

Oh shut up, all of you.

She slept. When she awoke she felt rested, replete. She had a feeling she'd been asleep a long time, and yet the sun had not yet risen to its zenith. She sensed something different in the movement of the boat. She went out on deck; many of the sails hung in tattered strips, the threads faded where they'd ripped. But three of the sails had been set, and were bellied full with the breeze. She looked at the pilot wheel, saw that it had been roped to the stanchion. The last time she'd looked it had spun aimlessly. Someone had set the sail and put the ship on course. To where? She didn't know, but the sun was now coming over the bow. Either they'd reversed directions, or it was afternoon instead of morning . . . .

Must have been Ewing, she thought. Or rather what I contain of Ewing, that helped me set the sails and turn the ship on a survival course.

She held out her hands and saw that they were calloused, the nails cracked. The thumb and forefinger of her right hand held the same brown-yellow stains she had noticed on Dawson. I've been smoking, too. Someone has been smoking. A titter escaped her lips and made her feel embarrassed. Steady girl. She went back in the Captain's cabin and looked in his round shaving mirror. The relief she felt at seeing her own face made her realize how near the edge she'd been. The sun had stained her to a darkness of mahogany. The green eyes looked cool as water, steady as stars. She was all right now.

And the bodies were gone. That unpleasant task had been delegated. No telling how many people she'd been. Judging from the darkness of her tan, she'd been out at least a week . . . .

Thinking of time made her hungry. She went into the galley and saw at once that she'd used it frequently. The little butane stove was spattered with grease, the sink piled high with dirty pots and skillets. Beside the sink was a garbage butt full of bones. Funny-looking bones. She stepped for a closer look, saw the seething maggots. Gah! The place stank of rotten meat. She decided to eat on deck. She opened the refrigerator and froze in shock. It was full of meat. Slabs of steak. Bowls of liver. She reached down at the bottom and took out what looked like a chicken drumstick. She studied it for a moment, then threw it to the floor with a gasp. "Thumb," she mused aloud, staring out the porthole. "I know it was a thumb. I saw the nail. There was a yellow stain, on the end, but most of the skin was bluish white from being boiled. And at the base of it there was . . . .

She looked down again. Most of the tattooed flower remained intact, but the word *Love* had been sliced neatly in half.

Dawson's thumb.

Where was the rest of him?

She gagged and tried to vomit, but the sickness was deeper than that. Her mind, made of dead people's thoughts. Her body, composite of the men she had eaten. She hated herself, hated the thing which controlled her. *Destroy it.*

She seized the butane tank and ripped it away from the stove. The gas dissipated through the portholes. She closed them all and fastened the clamps. When she could no longer bear the smell of gas, she struck a match and watched the flame spread out around the room like a blue bedspread. The concussion felt soft against her body, like someone oh so gently blowing out a candle . . . .

This would put an end to it. The fire would leave no flesh to be healed.

SIX

HER element was sea-foam, salt water and the multitude of swimming creatures who shared it with her. She had no idea how long she'd been in the water. The light came and went many times before she looked up at the gold coin in the sky and thought: *Sun.* Soon it was replaced by one of silver, floating in a purple-black sea. *Moon.* She had no idea where the sounds in her head came from, but there were more: *Star. Sky. Sea. Land.* The last word had nothing to do with the scalloped world of blue and white which she saw from the crest of a swell; land was green and rolling, with trees and cows. A tree was smooth on the bottom and fluffy on top. Cows were hairy things with thick curved spines growing out of their heads.

Every day when the sun came up she told herself she would remember something new. She liked some words better than others. *Mother* was soft and comforting; *Daddy* made her feel strong and sad at the same time. *Truck* was a twitch of fear and the vision of a big box on whining rollers. *Ship* was a word her mind shied away from; it brought chaotic flashes of fire, explosions, and a burning pain all over her body.

One day a flock of bright-colored birds flew over. Their green and purple plumage was a vivid contrast to the gray and white of the seabirds. Another day she heard the hollow boom of the surf. The waves began to lift her higher, and she saw the curving ranks of white marching in to surrender on the shining white-gold sand. Beyond that she saw the green fronds of coconut palms, and further back reared a purple mass larger than any wave she'd ever seen. Mountains. She felt excited at coming to land. There would be many new worlds to learn.

She was unprepared for the shock when her feet touched sand. Long-forgotten muscles came into play as she tried to stand; a breaking wave smashed her down against the harsh granules and somersaulted her amid white foam. It took several tries before she could swim in the bubbly white stuff, but at last she crawled up on the wet sand. She felt dizzy. The earth seemed to be swaying. Then she realized that her muscles, acclimated to the rhythm of the sea, had kept up their autonomic swimming motions. She got to her feet, surprised to see how far it was to the ground. She remembered how to walk; heel first, then toe, one foot before the other. It was easy. And the wind in her face. So much better than lying belly-down in the water, or floating on her back.

The sun felt stinging hot. She saw that her skin had become puckered, dry and scaly. The burning in her throat she identified as thirst. Must have taken water in through the skin, she thought, while I was swimming.

Bzzzzzz . . . click! The sound came from a little black box standing on three legs. As she approached it she saw that it was aimed down at a pebbled, star-shaped creature that had been stranded by the tide. She knew how it felt, the dryness beginning as an itch becoming needles of pain. She knelt down, planning to return the creature to its element.

"Don't touch it!"

He came running down the beach, black hair blowing out behind his ears, brown knees pumping inside cutoff blue jeans. He stopped ten feet away and stared at her. He wore old-fashioned rimless glasses. In one hand he held a partly-eaten oval fruit whose dripping juice made her throat ache.

"Did you move the camera? If you did the whole series is ruined."

Meaningless sounds beat at her ears. At first she did not connect them to the movement of his mouth, then she realized: *He was talking*. Such a complicated way to get the words into her head. She knew he was worried about the camera, and she sent him the message that everything was exactly as it had been. But he didn't respond, so she opened her mouth and awakened the dormant memory of speech.

"I . . . did . . . not . . . . " Suddenly bewildered, she began to sort through the cue words his mind was sending. *Touch. Bother. Move. Handle. Mess-with.*

He frowned. "You stoned or what? Here, hold this."

She took the slick fruit and felt the cool juice run down her fingers. She wanted to put it in her mouth, but hesitated because of the hostility he still radiated toward her. She watched him open the lid of the camera and look down into a square of glass. The clean brown wedge of his back gave her a sense of pleasure. She wanted to touch him, yet she had a feeling that if she did something unpleasant would happen.

"What are you photographing?"

"Life."

"That thing is dying."

He nodded without looking up. "That's part of life. Dying. To him, life is water." He straightened and looked at her. "What's life to you?"

She thought of Bari—a sense of forlorn longing mixed with the crash of gunfire on a stormy night. "Love."

"I knew you'd say that." He smiled for the first time. "Stark naked on the most desolate stretch of beach on the Pacific Coast of Mexico. Where'd you leave your clothes?"

"I don't know. I've been swimming a long time."

"Tripping too, aren't you?" He stepped closer and looked deep into her eyes. He stepped back shaking his head. "I just don't know—but I think you'd better stick with me for awhile. Some of the rancheros who live along here might misunderstand."

He took the mango from her hand and started walking. As they topped the line of dunes, she saw a vehicle parked under the trees beside a lagoon. A sleeping bag lay on a pile of grass, and a blackened earthenware pot simmered on a smouldering fire of coconut husks. "Been living off the land, sort of. Fruit, fish and coconuts. Clams and stuff." He pointed to a large movie camera set up on a tripod. "Making a one-man movie on jungle survival. My name's Verne, by the way."

"Anne." She said it without any sense of identity; it was only a label for the construction of bone and tissue she happened to inhabit.

He repeated the name, then knelt down and started adding more husks to the fire. "You hungry, Anne?"

"If I could have one of those fruits you were eating. . . . "

"Mango? Sure." From a straw basket he took an orange-yellow fruit, peeled back the leathery skin, and gave it to her. It oozed a thick sweet juice which she liked, despite the taste of turpentine. She saw that he was sprinkling green leaves on the surface of the boiling water. He took the kettle off the fire, set it on the sand, and laughed.

"This is too much. A girl comes down the beach wearing nothing but a locket on a chain, doesn't know where she's been or where she's going. So what do I do? I make tea. If I tried to film a plot like that, they'd say it was too ridiculous." He looked up at her, suddenly sober. "You've got a nice shape, but if it's all the same to you, I'll lend you a pair of pants and a shirt so you'll get it covered up. Okay?"

The fabric chafed her skin, but she liked the smell of sweat and tobacco which clung to the clothing. Verne seemed to relax once she had her body out of sight. As they drank tea, he said: "I was making skin flicks in southern Cal, no reason except to get the bread to come down here and do my own film. What I mean was, it just turned me off the physical scene entirely. I kept seeing you like that and I thought of work. A helluva hangup, but I'll get over it some day."

He went on talking as they walked the beach gathering driftwood for the fire. His philosophy reminded her of Bari's. When he mentioned the hungry children he'd filmed in a mining village, she asked: "Didn't you pity them?" He held up his left hand and said: "If I should cut this finger, would my right hand pity my left? No. I felt their pain and hunger."

Anne nodded, remembering a time when she had lived in constant hunger. Later, as Verne sliced potatoes and onions into a greased skillet, she felt the sharp edge of appetite, but nothing like the craving she remembered. I'm getting well, she thought. And then she wondered: How was I sick? She tried to recall, but there were impermeable barriers to her memory. She watched Verne whittle a point on a stick in order to husk a coconut, and she thought of David who had worn a steel claw. Why had he been looking for her? She didn't know, nor did she know why, when Verne sliced open a red fish and the blood oozed out, she could get a sick, vomiting feeling, mingled with the vision of a grease-spattered stove and the word *Love* scripted in blue letters.

That night he insisted she take his sleeping bag, while he rolled up in some blankets he took out of his Landrover. She found it hard to relax in the tight confines of the bag, but after she took off her clothes it wasn't too bad. She looked up at the stars and listened to Verne tell how he'd gotten into films while serving in the army signal corps. It made her think of uniforms and a musty hotel room. An electric sign blinked outside the window and something was sticking into her stomach . . . .

Better leave the past buried, she thought.

After breakfast, he had her hold the camera while he threw a purse net into the sea. He made a dozen fruitless casts before he halted, panting. "Damn lead weights wear me out. Care to try?"

She took the net and ran along the surf until she picked up the little nibbling fish-thoughts she'd lived with for so many months. Pivoting on the ball of her foot, she flung the net and drew it in by the cord. Caught in the nylon mesh were three flopping silver fish.

He took the camera from his eye and smiled. "You make me feel like a bunch of sticks put together with rusty nails. Such a smooth symmetry of motion, I get the feeling that space to you is a liquid medium, like water. Do something else. Open the net and throw the fish back in the water."

She was glad to do it, knowing the misery they felt. When she finished Verne capped his lens with a decisive movement. "Okay. You can be in my film if you like—I mean, if you have nothing else to do."

She had nothing. So he had her go through the motions of survival, gathering driftwood, building a fire. Walking in wet sand and digging up clams with her toes. Exploring the jungle, cutting bamboo shoots, digging arrowroot tubers along the lagoon. Cooking, eating, and of course, bathing in the lagoon.

"I want it to be natural," he said. "Nobody's around, so

you take a bath. Do it like you always do. I'll cut it out later if it looks like a peepshow routine."

She was momentarily conscious of her smooth breasts, no larger than a cupped hand, and recalled that she'd once carried great lumps of tissue of no more use to her than the curl on a pig's tail. She'd become streamlined for swimming. Now she hoped she'd never change back.

During the next week Verne treated her as a friend and a subject for filming. As they drove up the twisting sandy track which led to the thorn-covered hills, he said: "I'll mail this film from Uruapan, then I'm coming back to do some surfing. I'll give you enough money to get home on. You've earned more than that, but I won't have it until I get paid for this job—if I ever do."

She said nothing. There were dark and compelling reasons why she couldn't go back home, but they were lost in the caverns of forgetfulness. After a time he stopped the Landrover with a suddenness that slid all four wheels on the sand. She saw a three-foot lizard sitting on a log, his crested head posed majestically. His wrinkled neck was iridescent purple, shading to green on its back. She felt a tremor of fear. "What is it?"

"Iguana," said Verne, holding the whirring camera to his eye. "Common in these parts, but I never got one this big."

It was beautiful, she had to admit—yet she had a feeling of some monstrous evil. For an instant the jungle canopy became a beamed ceiling. She was in an underground room which smelled of ancient dust, and from the stone wall a single eye regarded her with loathing . . . .

She was glad when they drove on, though it was several minutes before the sunshine warmed the chill of her flesh.

In the city Verne seemed subdued, waiting in line at the post office, buying insurance for his film. Anne waited outside in the car, conscious of the curious sliding glances of the women and hard predatory gaze of the men. She felt uneasy about rejoining the world of people. Analyzing it she found that she was not worried about the essential of food, shelter and clothing, for these things had always been easy to acquire. No, the problem was in herself. Something evil was hiding in the dark spaces of her mind; she could feel it stirring, responding to the little tendrils of thought which leaked in from all sides. A man drove by in a Ford, grating his teeth as he honked at people and burros blocking his way; he glanced at her with narrow eyes, and she saw herself chained naked to a wall, while a steel whip drew blood from her back and spattered driplets on the stone floor. A ragged old woman came up and stretched out her hand, mumbling. Anne had no money. She looked at the old woman and shrugged; the vision came like the sudden clamp of a mousetrap, a thousand razor blades slicing open her skin, letting the juice ooze out of her body until she too was dried up, wrinkled and old. *Hate, hate. Is there nobody here who loves?*

She was glad to see Verne come out of the post office. He drove through the thronged streets to the bus station, stopped, and shut off the engine. His movements seemed slow and heavy. "I'll check the schedules, get your ticket. Where do you want to go?"

"Oh . . . anywhere. I don't care."

He looked straight ahead, drumming his fingers on the wheel. " 'I come like water and like wind I go.' Is that how you see it?" He laughed, but his face remained sober. "If you don't care, you could come back to the beach with me."

"I don't want to hang you up."

"No, listen." He turned to look at her. "When I met you, you said life is love. I never got around to asking you what love was. Now maybe we could get into it."

Love is surrender, she thought. So Bari had said. She felt warmth and trust when she thought of him. He had somehow lost his life because of her. And now this young man—so handsome, young and free, why did he want to change it? And why did she feel this sense of slipping, sliding, drifting into some kind of nightmare?

"All right," she said with reluctance. "Let's go back."

They did not return to the same beach, but went to a fishing village further down the coast. There a politician had built a deluxe three-story beach hotel in anticipation of a highway which had not yet left the drawing board. It had private balconies, a swimming pool and uniformed employees who stood on the polished steps with arms folded and glared as they passed by. Verne found a five-room *pension* with a thatched veranda overlooking the beach. A teenage boy played chess under a gas lantern with a man in his undershirt, who slapped his shoulders almost constantly with a rolled-up newspaper. Old bites pimpled his pale skin, and his flesh rippled with each blow.

They slept in the same bed that night, but when Verne lay his hand on her bare stomach she did not respond, so he took it away and went to sleep. Anne did not sleep, however; the warmth of the man beside her brought back memories of other males, of cheap wine and bristly whiskers, the sound of traffic and grunt of lovemaking in dark alleys. A hundred pairs of hands had gripped and kneaded her flesh, and for every pair she saw a face, and every face had a mouth which spoke her name: "Anne, I want . . . need . . . love . . . ."

But it was only Verne talking in his sleep.

Next morning, as they walked up the beach to find a private place to swim, he asked her why she'd been disinterested the night before. "I want to know if you were tired or . . . just didn't go in for that kind of thing, ever."

"I used to but . . . I quit."

"Why?"

"Well, it always turned out badly."

"When you say, 'turned out badly,' you mean you didn't enjoy it?"

"Oh yes. But the men died."

"Oh Christ!" He stopped and stared. "You mean you had a guy and he went off and got shot or something?"

"One got shot. Curt, his name was. Only I think he shot himself. Oh, there were two who got shot, if you count Ned. Barri would make three, only he never, we never . . . .

Verne laughed and slapped her rump. "You're building yourself up as a *femme fatale*, Anne. You just don't like to remember the men who went off and forgot you the next day."

He ran into the water and swam out beyond the surf. Anne sat down on the sand, fighting down an urge to follow him into the water. She wasn't sure she'd ever drum up the will to return to land. People seemed so frighteningly tender and soft, she could hardly move without hurting someone.

Verne ran out of the water and stretched out on the sand beside her. Droplets of water glistened in the hair on his chest.

"I've been thinking," she said. "There weren't any."

"Any what?"

"Any men who forgot me after they knew me. They're all dead, Verne."

He sat up and stared at her. "Jesus, you really believe it."

The subject was dropped, but it seemed to hover like a cloud. They planned to forage for food and cook supper on the beach, but three days of eating in restaurants had spoiled it for them. They planned to catch the sunset before returning to the hotel, but a cool wind sprang up and blew stinging sand against their legs. Verne shivered. "I think I'll go back and get something warm in my stomach. Come on, let's run."

The room was musty with the stale heat of the afternoon. Another smell raised the hair on Anne's neck. Verne wrinkled his nose. "Dead rat in here. I'll have him change the rooms."

Pepe, the manager, carried their bag to a room at the other end of the veranda. Ten minutes later, Verne looked up from tying his sneakers. "I smell it again. Must be a dead dog washed up on the beach."

They ate that night in a beach restaurant with a thatch roof. The kerosene lantern fluttered in the wind and gave off plumes of black oily smoke. Long shadows whipped across walls of woven palm ribs. Now and then a rat scurried across the rough-hewn beams overhead. Verne said they lived in the palm trees and kept themselves clean, but she noticed that he eyed them as warily as she did. She'd never seen him drink before, but tonight he had two rum cokes before the clam chowder, and another before the fried fish and potatoes. He stayed there drinking, even after the cook had doused her charcoal fire and gone home. His elbows developed a trick of sliding sideways every time he rested his chin on his hands. Around ten o'clock he peered at her from beneath sagging eyelids and muttered: "Let's go back to the room."

Her feet felt heavy as lead as they walked back. When they were in the room he stood watching her undress, swaying back and forth with his hands on his hips. "Well . . . ? "

"Good night." She pushed her feet under the sheet and

blew out the lamp. When she felt his hands on her she lay limp, neither resisting nor cooperating. It had turned him off the night before, but tonight he did not even hesitate. He rode her as he might have ridden his surfboard, treating her as an object which needed only to be present. After awhile she became aware that she was enjoying it. Sex was a pleasant way of combining male and female bodies, and not a venereal gorging to satisfy a demonic lust. She shifted her position to make herself more accessible to him. She had begun to adapt herself to his rhythm, to twist and bend in ways that increased the pleasant pressure when suddenly—

It was like a sack pulled over her head. She could not see or hear, or feel—yet in some remote corner of her mind she sat back and watched with horrified fascination, aware that her body was being controlled by another power. Certainly she—the one who watched—did not feel the emotions that tw.. the girl's face and bared her teeth so that they glistened like water in the moonlight, nor could she feel in any way responsible for the animal snarls that issued from her throat....

Afterward she could see herself lying limp with knees wide and hands relaxed palm up, the perfect stereotype of satiated womanhood. She thought: I must get back and straighten up my body. Then it was as if the alien presence reached back and pulled down the last curtain of absolute blackness—

Verne was shaking her. "Do you see it? *My God, do you see it?*"

She lifted her leaden head and stared into darkness. For a moment she thought she'd gone blind, then she realized there was no light in the room. The heavy smell of death was like a fetid blanket wrapped around her face.

"It's gone," he said. "It was just lying on the floor there, glowing. A blue radiance at the center, sort of burnt out at the edge. And then black patches, like—oh, they were black, blacker than black. Like holes in the void."

It took an effort to get the words past her lips. "Are you sure?"

"What the hell. Sure I'm sure. I never hallucinated like that. Even when I could smell, touch and see a thing, I've always been able to say to myself, wow, what a hallucination. You know? But this one—it was something else."

"There are different levels of hallucination."

"I know. And I'll tell you something else. This life is an hallucination. We're born and we die and the whole scene is an ego trip. But even knowing this—I was scared. This thing was from somewhere else." He groped around, lit a match, and the lamp went on. She saw the sweat gleaming on his face as he tipped the rum bottle and drank. "Something I couldn't possibly ever dream of. I told you what it looked like but vision is only a small part of it. Just to give you an idea of that cold thing waiting, totally without emotion, squatting, monstrously malevolent. Hell, I can't describe it. I had the feeling I could die, and that would be no help, no help whatever. Because this thing reached over the line that separates life and death. Oh hell, I gotta get out of here."

She watched him pull on his pants and shirt. "I think it came from me, Verne."

He looked at her a minute. "Yeah, maybe." He turned away and did not meet her eyes. "I'll be back in a little while, soon as my head clears up." He started out, then came back and picked up the bottle by the neck. He didn't look at her as he walked out, and she had a feeling he would not be back.

A few minutes later she heard the Landrover's engine start, followed by a rattle of gears and the grating of tires. She heard him roar up the main street of the village, slow down for the crossing, then spin out onto the pitted road leading across the coastal plain. Even after he passed beyond the range of her hearing, she had flickering glimpses of his headlights on the neat cribbage pattern of the coconut trees. A long time later she saw deep jungle shadows and vines like snakes writhing in moonlight. Suddenly she felt a jangling sense of horror, a fear of death. Her body went rigid on the cot. A blinding flash of light spread out and suffused her entire being and then . . . .

Peace. She slept.

It rained every day for the next three weeks. Anne ate a little, but never felt hungry. She knew Verne would not return now, since all roads were flooded between the coast and the mountains.

The manager of the hotel spoke passable English. He taught her to play chess, but usually they sat on the patio practicing Spanish and watching the rain drip off the thatch. Everything sprouted a gray-green mould. The fishing boats rarely went out, and those that did returned empty, for the runoff from the rains had driven the fish offshore. The fishermen stayed in the cantinas and drank; there were many fights, but Anne thought that was normal. One night two men were knifed in the alley behind the hotel. Several shots were fired, women were screaming and men were shouting, but Anne thought she dreamed it all. She only learned it was real the next morning when the manager came to her room and told her with a shamefaced expression that she was being blamed for it.

"I was asleep. How could I do anything?"

He spread his hands and shrugged. "Women talk. They say there was no violence before you came. They call you *bruja.* Evil witch. Even my own *señora* . . . . "

Anne felt as though the gray-green fungus had grown inside her mind. She found it hard to stir herself to action, but she managed to walk to the jetty and arrange passage to Acapulco with the captain of the supply ship. He took what remained of the money Verne had given her and said he would leave at six p.m. At five she stood on the beach and watched his stubby craft pass the lighthouse and chug out into the open sea.

Strange things happened. A sea-turtle was netted and hauled to the village market. The fish-vendor cut it open and began selling eggs out of its belly. In a post-mortem convulsion it lifted its head and bit off his hand. A dam in the hills which supplied the village with fresh water overflowed and burst, covering three homes with silt. Twelve women and children died. After that there was no fresh water in the town. There was only one well, and the people who drank from it got sick.

None of this seemed to have anything to do with Anne. She could feel herself putting on weight, and each day it took a greater effort to move from her bed to the veranda. Pepe's *señora* was a thin hawk-eyed woman with a voice like a guacamaya; she shrieked at the servants until they all quit, then she turned on Pepe. The woman had learned that the ship captain had taken all Anne's money and she demanded that Pepe throw her out. Pepe refused, and after a fight which attracted every idler on the beach, the woman moved out.

Anne knew she was agitating against her. On the rare days when the rain stopped, she liked to sit in the little park in front of the post office. Once the children had played around her and asked for money. Now they hid behind bushes and watched her. The bravest threw rocks.

Floods had driven dozens of feral dogs out of the lowlands to the beach, where they ran in fierce packs. One family returned from a visit to the store and discovered that something had gotten into their shack and killed two children. Some said it could not have been dogs, since the bodies were uneaten, but wild dogs had been seen in the area, so it was against these that the men took action. They killed a cow and poisoned the meat with strychnine; for nearly a week the howls of dying dogs echoed in the night, and the smell of death hung like a cloud over the beach. Anne no longer went swimming, for the rotting carcasses churned endlessly in the surf. Vultures perched on the benches of the park. Anne stopped walking in the village, because people turned away from her and crossed themselves. Even the village *padre,* a blue-eyed young man who'd grown haggard from sanctifying rooms and conducting funerals, began avoiding her.

Then Pepe died. Anne knew it when she awakened at dawn with the dying echo of a scream in her ears. The nightmare had been like many others she'd had recently: The abrupt clamping-off of all her senses, followed by a sensation of floating through dark streets. Often she'd seen faces twisted in terror or frozen with fear. Tonight it had been Pepe's.

Now she lay listening to the distant shouts. She perceived that the rain had stopped, but the trees and the thatch continued the steady drip-drip-drip which had gone on for weeks. She remembered playing chess with Pepe the night before, and had noticed that he wore a gun in a holster clipped to his belt. Why? "They are trying to kill me. I don't know what. Last night something tried to smother me in my sleep. Your move."

She knew he had held back the anger of the villagers; now it would be unleashed. She got up and gathered her few possessions, rolled them in a sheet, and went out the back gate of the hotel. The *padre* was walking toward her, leading a black horse without a saddle. He was barefoot, his face ghostly under his wide-brimmed black hat. Silently he pointed to the horse, and she climbed on.

Faces peered from doorways as he plodded down the street ahead of her, holding the reins of the horse. She felt their fear and their hatred; she saw visions of herself tied to a stake with the flames licking her body, but nobody came out. Low clouds hung over the village; the air was heavy and warm and pungent with the smell of death and growing things.

At the crossroads he put the reins in her hands. "You know that Pepe is dead?"

"Yes."

"I do not ask how you know. I am an educated man. I have no superstition. He ran from the hotel to the beach and fell dead. The boy who discovered the body said that something was on him, eating. He could not describe it." He gave a sad apologetic smile. "It was dark, of course. And the body was unmarked. But his story is believed. Here the people always seek an outside cause for their troubles, rather than look into their hearts and find the evil therein. *Pues bein.* You simply stay on the road. There is danger in the jungle, but your chances are better than here. *Vaya con Dios.*"

She rode all day, and that evening she came to a river. She had a feeling, as she guided the horse down the sloping bank, that she had been here before. She slid off, tied the reins to a sapling, and started walking through the dripping ferns which grew along the bank. She had no idea where she was going, but she had a sense of being guided. Driven was a better word. She had complete control of her body, but each time she turned way from the river, her mind jangled and her flesh crawled until she groped her way back. She thought of psychologists guiding a rat by means of electrified grids. She knew the helpless curdling rage the rat must feel, the desperate urge to understand what was wanted, so that no more shocks would come.

Then she saw the Landrover, trapped in the giant roots

of a fallen eucalyptus tree. Silt covered it to the bottom of the windshield. The roof was alive with gray-green mould, and a strangler fig had taken possession of the chassis. It was not hard to understand what had happened. Verne had tried to ford the river, had missed the raised portion in the darkness, and was swept away by the rising river. But how had he died? She couldn't tell. His skeleton still sat behind the wheel, held upright by drifted silt. His moss-covered skull mocked her with its ivory smile. She felt no emotion at all, just a bone-weary despair.

I am here, she thought. Minutes passed, and she could feel the earth turning beneath her feet. Finally she screamed: *"What do you want? Tell me what to do!"*

The jungle seemed shocked and dismayed by her outburst. The vines, the leaves, the trees all had little eyes which stared at her. The plants whispered among themselves, insulting her. The skull grinned, and Verne's teeth glowed in the darkness. *You were supposed to love me,* she thought. But there was no love inside an empty skull.

She felt herself dissolving. She saw her flesh fall away from her body. She reached down with a boney hand and pinched the gleaming white femur of her leg. It crumbled like yeast, and laughter echoed through the trees. Who was laughing? Not her. She didn't exist. She had been eaten by the monster, there was nothing left of Anne.

SEVEN

Dr. Alvin Duffy wondered how the woman managed to project such svelte refinement in a mental home—even an exclusive 500-dollars-a-week establishment like the Desert Rest. She sat in the studio-living room of her private apartment, legs crossed, the hem of her skirt revealing the six inches of sheathed leg which modesty permitted for that particular year. Through the floor-to-ceiling window Duffy could see a Japanese garden with stone lantern and arching bridge across the pool, and grass growing down to the water's edge. He watched the fountain go through its cycle; first a single jet shooting straight up from the center, then seven smaller jets in a circle around it, then a third larger ring composed of—he estimated quickly—forty-nine jets. The display culminated in a vast umbrella of spray, then the jets cut off, one ring at a time, until there was only a lone little spurt at the center.

"How long is the cycle?" he asked.

"Four and one-half minutes," she said. Her eyes slid over to him. They were the strangest eyes he had ever seen. Almond-shaped, they moved with the magical swiftness of oil spreading on water. The deep clear green of the iris, the blueish skim-milk color of the whites—all this seemed only an overlay. Beneath it the dark blot of the pupil spread out and encompassed all, so that no matter which direction she faced, he had the feeling of being under her scrutiny. The sensation he felt was that of a little boy caught in a lie, sheepish and guilty but at the same time relieved of the need to pose as a man.

"But this is not getting my work done," he said at last.

"What is your work?" she asked.

"I, uh, have this grant." For some reason he felt like laughing at himself. "I'm doing a study on people who adapt to life in institutions."

"What kind of institutions?"

I'm supposed to be asking the questions, he thought. "All kinds," he answered. "I've already visited several prisons. My interest centers on those who behave as model prisoners inside the walls, but who, once outside, immediately commit some sort of crime which leads them right back in. I've surveyed the military—professional career men, 'lifers' they're called, who submit to the army's harsh discipline rather than think for themselves. I've also surveyed the inmates of the state mental institutions who seem unable to adapt to life outside, but who, so to speak, find a home in the institution."

"And now you come down to us."

"Well, *you*, to be specific. The others here—child molesters and senile pederasts who in their prime were captains of commerce—alkies, addicts and freaked-out misfits from the best families—the only difference between them and the state hospital inmates is money. But you weren't put here by relatives or committed by the authorities. You ____." He glanced at his notebook. "Appeared five y___ ago dressed fashionably and expensively, in a leased limousine complete with chauffeur. You presented a cashier's check for the first year, an amount close to thirty thousand dollars. You demanded that no medicines be given you and no drugs except for mild sedatives, upon request. You requested extensive security measures to be undertaken at your expense, bars and steel doors and alarm systems, and that no contact be permitted between you and the other inmates—guests, rather. All are symptoms of paranoid schizophrenia, except for one anomalous factor. They weren't designed to keep other people from hurting you, but to keep you from hurting other people."

He saw that she was watching him with an amused smile flickering around her lips. For a second he felt like a pompous idiot, and had to remind himself that he was thirty-one years old, a Ph.D. *magna cum laude,* with a reputation for brilliance in his chosen field. "I'm sorry. Did you have a question?"

"Yes. What is it you want from me?"

"I would like to conduct a series of interviews with you, find out where you differ from the others I've studied."

"I differ from the others? In what respect?"

"For the most part, these are, well, I'll tell you frankly, they're gravy-brained meatheads who have no thoughts except those which are put into their heads. In any society they will sell their freedom, and the freedom of everybody else, down the river to any power-hungry demagogue who promises them that they can eat and sleep warm and wend their straight and narrow path to the grave without ever having to think, or to take any action which has not been programmed in advance and laid out for them by someone else." He saw that she was smiling again, so he broke off his tirade. "But you are bright, intelligent, quick-witted. You show capability of thinking for yourself. You could, I think, rise quickly to the top of the social structure that prevails outside these walls. Yet you have chosen to isolate yourself from humanity as effectively as if you were marooned on an island. Why?"

"Suppose I told you that I was inhabited by a being which now and then takes over my body and forces me to commit dark and evil deeds."

There was a long silence. At last he found his voice. "If you told me that I would laugh."

"You aren't laughing."

He was aware that his hands had begun to perspire. "Are you presenting it as the truth?"

"It could be."

"But is it?"

There was a long silence, which she broke by rising from her seat. "How many interviews do you require for your study?"

"Ten is the normal number."

"How often?"

"You're the only one I'm interested in here. We could do it daily, and be finished in two weeks."

"All right. Then I'll see you again tomorrow."

She walked to a wall panel and pressed a button. A televised image of the nurse appeared on the screen. "Yes, ma'am?"

"Doctor Duffy is leaving now. He's to be allowed in again tomorrow at two p.m." She cut off the screen without waiting for an acknowledgement, touched Duffy's hand lightly with her fingers, and walked out into the miniature walled garden. She knelt beside the pool and remained frozen like a stone image. He watched her for several minutes before he became aware of a buzzer behind him. A red light winked and a door was opening onto the long paneled corridor which led to the outside world. Duffy went, reflecting that this was one of the strangest women he'd ever seen. The back of his hand still tingled where her fingers had touched.

Next day he set the microphone on the coffee-table between them, leaned back, and lit a cigarette. She sat on the couch with one knee crossed over the other, her flowered silk lounging pajamas flaring out around her ankles.

"The tape recorder won't inhibit you?" he asked.

"No."

He flicked a switch that started the tape reels turning. "I want the complete story of your life. Let's begin with what are commonly known as the vital facts. What is your full name?"

"Anne."

He waited, but nothing more was forthcoming. "You prefer not to give your full name? Is it well known?"

"No."

"I see." He looked at her, wondering if she were lying. He could return to the name later. "Your age then."

She was silent a moment, then she laughed softly. "I seem to have two answers to that. I don't think you'd believe either one."

"What are they, please?"

"First answer: I'm eighteen."

"Hmmm. In appearance you could pass. But your manner is more appropriate to a woman of thirty-five. What was the second answer?"

"Twelve hundred and forty-two. Years."

He looked at her for a long time. One of the reels on the recorder squeaked faintly, and he made a mental note to squirt on some graphite. Finally he said: "Is this along the line of that comment you made about being inhabited? That is, you don't know whether it's true or not?"

"Yes."

"Why did you say years? What else could it be?"

"The concept isn't clear. Some other way of measuring time. . . ."

She trailed off, and he decided to prompt her. "Our way of measuring time is with celestial bodies. A year is one revolution around the sun. A day is one rotation of the earth on its axis. I suppose we could use other standards: the length of time it takes a bean to sprout, or an ice cube to melt . . . ."

"This has nothing to do with movement or processes. It's the difference between looking at a piece of spaghetti from the inside, and from the outside. But we'd better pass that now."

"All right. Fine." He shifted his feet and coughed. "This other age you gave, eighteen? That means you came here at thirteen. With a cashier's check for thirty thousand? Impossible. There's one thing about this place—they don't give a damn if you're Adolf Hitler as long as the check is negotiable, but they know a thirteen-year-old girl can't legally commit herself anywhere in this country. You gave your age as twenty-five, which would make you thirty now. I'll believe that—but not eighteen."

"If we're to get anywhere you must accept what I say as the truth. Otherwise there's no point in taking this down, is there?"

"All right then. Explain it."

"I was normal until I was eleven. Then I suddenly grew very fast."

"You know exactly when it started?"

"The day my father died."

"Hmmm. Death of a parent could speed up the maturation of personality, yes. But nothing physical. You say this was physical?"

"Yes. I started eating a lot. Then I noticed I was growing. Not until I ran away did I realize I had an insatiable craving for sex."

Despite himself, he glanced down at her legs, noting the firm pressure of flesh against the fabric. Looking up again, he caught the fading flicker of a smile. "Insatiable?"

"At that time, yes. Since then the urge has left me."

"A pity." He shook his head, then smiled. "You ran away at thirteen and I suppose you took a lover—to use the archaic term."

"Lovers. I told you I was insatiable."

"Oh yes. Well, suppose you give me a brief resume—hat you remember about them, how the affairs terminated . . . . "

"Well, the first was Hubert. I thought he was nice and big and strong. The affair ended because he died, when his truck got out of control on a hill. Then came the two boys in a Mercedes. I thought they left me, but they had a wreck too. Then Curt. He said he'd come back but he shot himself. He had a flavor of lemons and salt. Then Luis, who drove a tanker into a concrete wall. He was tender, but wild and gamey . . . . "

"You think of men in terms of food?"

"I think I did, 'way back at the beginning."

"And now?"

"I don't think of them at all."

"All right. After Luis, there was . . . . "

"Ned and Wilma. She shot him and then herself. Next the cadets. Somebody told me later there were six, but I wasn't counting at the time. Then there were some migrant workers in a truck, I think one was named Barney but I don't recall the others. And the men who picked me up hitch-hiking, some of them didn't introduce themselves. I get them mixed up now: Harold Clair, a man who said he was Doctor Bradley, a man named Smith, no there were two John Smiths . . . . "

An hour later he shut off the recorder and packed his tapes. He knew he'd play it back again and again, and he wondered if repetition would make it any more believable. In any case, he might get a hint of what she was concealing behind this unusual fantasy.

During the next two sessions he began to detect the shape of three distinct personalities. On the surface she was a urbane, self-contained woman. Beneath that she was a young girl, sometimes gay and sometimes sad, depending on the memory she was narrating. Still deeper was the mood she revealed when she spoke of the creature inhabiting her: then her voice took on a styrofoam flatness, like someone reading the fine print on an insurance policy.

"When was the first time you thought of this obsession pattern as being a creature apart?"

"It was when the man died in the truck-camper in the desert. It seemed like something was standing behind me, looking over my shoulder, forcing me to stay and watch him die."

"Before that—what did you feel when somebody died? Ned and Wilma, for example?"

"I felt no emotion at all. Just a deep sort of despair. Or not despair exactly. Just a suspicion that everything I touched . . . died. Then with the cadets I remember thinking they were going to die, but I saw them being shot down in flames."

"And the first time you ever deliberately seduced a man, knowing he would die?"

"That would be Dawson. On the yacht."

"But you told yourself it was to save Bari."

"Well there was always a rationalization. Only with the drunks it couldn't hold up. I knew I was on a death trip, and I tried to figure a way out. I was doing that when David showed up."

"How did you feel about David?"

"Very strange. Like he was standing behind warped glass. I felt he was very important to me, but I was puzzled because it didn't seem like it was time. I felt like you do when the guest of honor arrives an hour early at the party. You want to treat him well, but you really have no use for him at the moment."

"You think David is alive?"

"Oh yes. I'd know if he were dead."

So strange, he thought as he drove to his apartment, that such a lovely cultured woman (and she'd obviously read the books which filled one wall of her living room) could sit and clamly describe lying in the gutter with some whiskery old drunk. He could see it all too vividly: scrawny old blue-veined legs beneath a ragged overcoat streaked with dried vomit, Anne's smooth white hands holding him . . . .

By the end of the week, she occupied most of his thoughts. The prospect of not seeing her again until Monday dismayed him.

"So many promising avenues are opening up," he told her, "it would be a shame to risk breaking our *rapport*. Suppose I came in tomorrow—or I have a chalet in the mountains south of Flagstaff . . . why are you smiling?"

"You want to take me there, is that it?"

"I think a change of setting would be helpful."

She rose and pressed the buzzer. When the nurse appeared on the screen, she said: "Come in and pack my bags. I'm going away with Doctor Duffy."

A uniformed doorman was there to put her bags in the trunk of Duffy's car. As he drove north through the desert, he asked: "Where'd you get all the money, by the way?"

"Mr. Haverill's key. He'd put away more than he thought—over a million. I haven't used much."

A million. Fortunately his motives were honest. What if some shrewd gigolo got hold of this naive woman . . . .

He noticed that she was smiling again. "I see. You read minds."

"It's rarely worth the trouble, believe me."

Yes, he thought, but the ability is there. On second thought, he decided to feel sorry for the hypothetical gigolo . . . .

The chalet was a modern one with redwood siding; the large living room overlooked a forested valley with a stream cascading down the center. A half-dozen plumes of smoke betrayed the presence of other habitations, but the nearest was a mile distant. Duffy carried her bags into the smallest of the two bedrooms, then unpacked the groceries and put two steaks in the broiler. By the time he lit the candles and poured the wine, the purple shadow of night had consumed the valley, while the topmost peaks glowed red in the setting sun. Anne sat across from him in a black velvet dress; the neckline plunged out of sight beneath the table.

"Did you ever see your family again?" he asked.

She shook her head without raising her eyes from the task of dividing her steak into precise one-inch squares. "My mother knows I'm alive and well. The rest of it she wouldn't believe. I deposited some money in a bank, and they send her a monthly check."

"It's a decent and human thing to do," he said.

She looked at him. "You're mocking me."

"In a sense. For one who is inhabited by a monster—I assume we're still operating under that pretense? Well, you seem unusually warm and personable, and if I may say, lovable."

Soberly, she said: "I think I'm supposed to be."

"What does *that* mean?"

"Before, I was an uncommonly ugly and nasty girl. Wouldn't it be ridiculous to give me an attractive body, then leave me with a personality that turned men off? No, it's part of the game, to be lovable."

Duffy took a sip of red wine and observed the flickering shadow of the candlelight between her breasts. "Everything fits, of course. All facts must be whittled down, pruned and shaped to fit your delusion, or else forgotten. Your life story proves that you are inhabited by a supernatural power, but only to someone who refuses to doubt. Men died? Well, men die all the time. You've got a strong character and a high sexual voltage—so high in fact that you could induce psychotic reactions in certain kinds of men. So that a kid might drive off the road. Another might be so depressed he'd put a gun to his head. Another might have an attack of delerium tremens and drive into a river. Old men with *angina pectoris* would suffer seizures. Alcoholics with rotten livers and enlarged hearts would hemorrhage. This monster is a product of your own mind. Your belief is what's eating you, and believe me, it's no less a disease than if you had spirochetes in your bloodstream."

"Cure me then." She lay down her fork with a square of steak still impaled on the tines. "And you can have my million."

"I will." He held her gaze until her face faded and blended with the wavering shadow on the wall behind her. Then he dropped his eyes. "But I don't want your money."

Nothing more was said until they were seated before a crackling fire of dry birch logs. Duffy sipped his Drambuie and thought: *If she ever really convinced people, they'd try to kill her. It would be instinctive.* He thought how vulnerable she looked, seated on the hassock beside the fireplace, her long white neck bowed as she gazed into the fire. The heavy poker hung behind her on its peg. How easy it would be . . . .

"It's been tried."

She spoke in a flat tone without lifting her head. The knowledge that she'd picked up his thoughts threw him off-balance, but he recovered quickly. He'd noted the talent in others, though Anne was the first person he'd met who used it as a functional tool.

"I remember—the boy with the bayonet. May I see the scar?"

"There's nothing to see. It's all healed."

"You see how you caulk up the leaks in your illusion? You had to explain why you didn't die, so you invented this marvelous healing power."

"Shall we test it?" She got up smoothly. "I'll get a knife—"

"No. No!" He had a vision of blood spraying from an unstaunchable wound—which would be only slightly worse than if it didn't. He felt relieved when she resumed her seat. "The scientific method is to assume that a theory is true and then test it—but not at the risk of destroying the subject. Now let's say you harbor this creature. Attempts at suicide would be thwarted by the occupant, assuming it can exercise momentary control over your body. This would lead to a war between the two egos for possession of your body." He lifted his glass, proud of the oiled precision of his brain. "After deciding that you couldn't kill yourself, I suppose your next move would be to cut yourself off from humanity in an attempt to starve the creature out. Am I right?"

"Yes."

"But this would be thwarted by the creature, and its hunger would drive you into the open again."

"As it happens. Right again, Doctor Duffy."

He studied her. "You feel that you were driven out?"

"Lured out, I'd say."

"By whom?"

"*You* made it sound so attractive . . . ."

A moment later her meaning sank in. "You're saying the monster has taken control of *me* in order to lure *you*." He felt breathless. "It's too far-fetched, really." He stood up to pour another Drambuie, but the room tilted abruptly. "I think I'd better have a cold swim."

Behind the cabin Duffy had dynamited a pool out of

solid rock to catch the stream which trickled down from a snow-cap. He undressed in his bedroom, slid open the glass door, and made a running leap into the pool. The icy water shocked his nervous system to full alertness; he puffed and splashed across the ten-foot width and crawled out on the opposite side, his body burning with cold. A light flashed on in the spare bedroom, which had a picture-window looking out onto the pool. He watched her unzip the dress in back and push it down to the floor, stepping out of it with the grace of one performing a minuet. Duffy's view of her slender white body was marred only slightly by black silk panties that looked less substantial than smoke.

The light went out, and Duffy became aware that he crouched wet and shivering on the cold stones. He ran into his bedroom, toweled himself with masochistic savagery, and put on flannel pajamas. Back in the living room, he sipped a cup of freshly brewed coffee and recited in his mind the two cardinal rules he'd adopted while still in pre-med:

One: *Never accept the patient's delusion.*

Two: *Avoid emotional involvement.*

It was time for a little objective study. He got out the tapes he'd made of the interviews, set up the recorder, and settled the earphones on his head. Her voice filled his head with its clear musical lilt. When she came to the death of Verne he stopped the tape and wrote in his notebook: *Point out to Anne that she was in her bed when Verne ran into the river, thus had nothing to do with his death. Her probable response will be that the creature has developed a talent for controlling another person over long distance . . . .*

He stopped writing and lifted his head. Was that a splash? He went out and looked into the pool; an octopus stain of dark ink seemed to be floating on the surface. He reached behind him and flicked a switch. The floodlights revealed only clear, glittering water. It had been a shadow.

He went back into the living room and wrote: *There would be no need for the creature to take direct control of one's body. By producing a visual hallucination, it could induce the desired reaction without detection. Thus I might be persuaded to believe that the draperies were on fire. I would naturally start throwing water on them, or perhaps rip them down and carry them outside at a dead run. A third party, seeing no fire, would assume I'd gone mad. To me, the action would be the epitome of common sense.*

He yawned suddenly and closed his eyes. Immediately he fell asleep, and dreamed that he went into Anne's room. On the floor lay a black bladder the size of a football; he started to pick it up and it began swelling until it filled the room. He tried to get out but there was nothing but a great fog of soot and a red eye in the center.

He woke up sweating. When he looked into Anne's room he saw that she was sleeping with her palms together, fingertips touching her chin in an attitude of prayer. She looked like a girl of fourteen, innocent, pure and untouched.

Next day when they walked through the woods, butterflies fluttered in the glade and sunbeams speared down through the tall conifers.

He said as she unpacked the lunch: "I've got a theory which might cover this beast of yours. Want to hear it?"

"Yes."

"Point one." He lifted a drumstick. "Man is part of nature. Point two: Nature is constantly in balance. This balance is maintained by interlocking cycles of death. Big ones eat little ones, from the whale right down to the praying mantis. Point three: Man as a predator has apparently upset the balance, but in the nature of things, he must also be a victim. Question: Who is man's predator?"

Anne popped half a deviled egg in her mouth and wiped her fingers in the forest litter. "Man himself."

"That would make man the only self-limiting species in existence, and I don't think we're that special."

"Well, micro-organisms, germs and parasites."

"No. Man is incidental to these. They are not specifically directed against man, but attack animals too. Anyway these are parasites, or symbiotes. Not predators."

"Cancer? A cell growth inside man. Runaway tissue?"

"Here again animals have it. No. I'm thinking of something which feeds off man, and man exclusively. It doesn't necessarily have to be large, but I think it should be intelligent. Perhaps of a different order of intelligence than man. Nor does it have to have been around a long time. Predators develop when the prey grows plentiful. For example take the development of large land reptiles. As they grew bigger, the predators did also. Size was their major development, so the predator merely outdid them in size. The whole trend culminated in Tyrannosaurus Rex. And what happened? Placental mammals. Little innocuous creatures, running around under the feet of these huge behemoths, developed quickness, cleverness. They hit the reptiles where they were the weakest, that is, in their adaptability. Ate their eggs, for one thing. And little by little, replaced the reptiles in all their ecological niches."

She looked at the chicken wing, frowned for a moment, then crushed the breaded crust with her teeth. "What would this super-predator eat?"

"Well, not flesh, otherwise it would be easier to eat other animals. I'm not sure it *would* eat, in the sense that we know it. I think it preys on man for something nonmaterial, something uniquely human."

"I've read that man is the only animal with a sense of self-awareness."

"That's it!" Duffy pointed the gnawed drumstick at her as if it were a pistol. "I-dentity. The ego. The opinion, *I am.*"

Anne frowned. "But it seems like an intellectual concept."

"More than that. The sense of identity is the *sine qua non* of competitive man. We have our institutions full of people who have lost it. They would, many of them, die without the shelter of the institution. In its deepest sense, it provides for the survival of the body. Without the 'I' sense hunger would be undirected, impossible to satisfy. Thirst, sex-drive, all these things are funneled through the key-hole of direct individual experience. Picked over and examined by the I-sense." He paused for a bite of potato salad, then went on. "Each person is a unique blend of heredity and experience. To the predator each person would have a unique flavor. Some bland, some tart, some bitter. During its early development, the creature would probably eat anything that came its way, like a teenager. But as it grew up, its taste would become jaded, demanding more not quantity, but quality. It would become selective about its human diet."

She was silent so long that he asked: "What are you thinking?"

"Oh, carrying on the analogy. As a gourmet it would flavor the food by adding little spices of its own. So it might try to change the victim's personality, or enrich it somehow —say, by causing the victim to fall in love with the host. Then, when the morsel was flavored and properly cooked, it would . . . eat." She laughed slightly as she poured coffee out of the thermos.

"Are you speaking from personal experience?"

"I guess. I was thinking at the beginning I just wanted every man that came along. Later on I met some I didn't like. I don't know . . . on the ship I think I wanted the captain, but there were problems involved so I took Dawson."

"You took them all, didn't you? Except for the crewmen who got away?"

"You mean when they died?"

"Yes."

"Not Bari."

"Why not Bari?"

"I couldn't find him. As a yogi his ego was compressed, controlled, narrowed down to a needle-point. I don't think he died. I think he just . . . became me, and hid in there and then when I was cast adrift on the sea he just took over. All the things he'd learned about body control, they became mine. I couldn't swim that well, but Bari could. And he had this talent for going into other people's minds. I picked that up. And the graceful way he moved . . . I remember Verne mentioning that on the beach. I was never so graceful before."

She did have a feline grace, he thought as he watched her pack the picnic things. When she excused herself and went behind a mossgrown boulder, he reflected that she had played with him like a cat, pretending to discuss theory while telling him: *Be careful, I am going to eat you.* Well, it was natural for the subject to try to draw the analyst into her delusion. There would be ego-conflict ahead, he could see that. He could also see, as she rose from behind the rock and stood poised at that moment when a woman is most awkward, with pants at half-mast and bare buttocks protruding, that the contest would not be mere joust of the minds. She knew her most powerful weapon was sex, and she had the intelligence to play the game at its highest level.

Later, as they took a swim in his pool to wash off the accumulation of sweat and grime, he noticed that the icy water produced goosepimples on her flesh. Why wouldn't the creature suppress them, if it controlled her? But then he thought: Of course. They're attractive. The texture they give to her breasts, and those little white nodules around the aureoles.

"If what you say is true," he said, "the damn thing's invulnerable."

"Why so?" She was drying her feet, pulling the towel back and forth between her toes.

"Well, the creature would undoubtedly learn to select as host the people most likely to command the greatest ease of contact with the opposite sex. I'm assuming some kind of virus or death-wish is transmitted during intercourse. So, if it took over a female, she would be the loveliest, sexiest, most seductive wench in town. The description fits you. If male, it would be the type most sought-after in our society: handsome, strong, rich, successful.

She lifted her head and stared at him. "If male? You think there are men like me?"

"It seems logical."

"I wonder . . . . " She toweled herself absent-mindedly, rubbing her sex as casually as if she were in her own bedroom. He noticed that the sun brought a reddish tint to the tight-curled hair and shined its way down the division of flesh so enticing that he wondered if he would care if she were a monster or not.

"What do you wonder?" he asked.

"If I would know." As if suddenly aware that her motions had taken on a masturbatory flavor, she started toweling her arms with vigor. "When I met one, I mean. Would we know each other? If so, what would we do? Shake hands and say, Well how's it going, getting plenty to eat?" She gave him an upward-slanting look which was both coy and accusing. "Are you one, by chance?"

He laughed to cover an attack of self-consciousness. "I seem to have the qualifications: handsome, strong, intelligent, attractive to the opposite sex . . . . Hey, don't look at me that way. I'm only kidding."

She continued to stare until he thrust out his feet and

pushed her into the pool. He was glad when she shrieked, it was such a reasurring, feminine sound.

Anne went to bed soon after supper, saying that she was tired. Duffy sat listening to his tapes for an hour or so, then he got his notebook and started writing:

Such a creature would find it easy to camouflage itself in our so-called 'rational' society. Belief in supernatural possession is the mark of a superstitious fool, thus many incidents would go unreported by people afraid of embarrassment. All deaths must be classified under one or another bureaucratic heading: homicide, suicide, accident, disease. Having one's ego devoured by a demon is unacceptable. It must be more difficult for the creature to function in primitive settings, where people have no hesitation about accepting the supernatural. Witness Anne's trouble in Mexico, where the villagers quickly identified her as the causal agent. Apropos, one wonders why the creature does not avoid placing the host in jeopardy simply by controlling its appetite. Possibly it goes out of its head with greed, like a gastrophage on an eating binge. This brings into question its intelligence. Possibly it is a moron by human standards, insensate as a tick on a dog's ear . . . .

He raised his head and stared into the fire. Such a creature did not deserve Anne. He would operate on her psyche with the scalpel of his intellect; he would cut the worm from the apple.

He yawned and closed his eyes. The warmth of the fire made him drowsy.

When he awoke the fire had died. His hand felt cramped where it held the pen. He looked down at his notebook and read:

I am neither a higher power nor a lower power—but an alternate power. I do not seek to justify myself. I am. I have appetite. Better said, I am my appetite.

I do not know the origin of my species, no more than man knows the origin of his. We are not gregarious. When I scent the markings of others, I depart. Except for breeding, we avoid each other. As the population of man increases, we increase. Sometimes by accident we overbreed and men rise against us. It has happened.

I write this for a purpose, Duffy. To make you afraid. At present you have the sweet vulnerability of youth, marinated in the over-indulgence of your mother. Your father's strictness provided the lean toughness of your mind. The sibling rivalry with your brother gives a tang. The spice of fear will blend the flavors, and the knowledge of your approaching death

There it ended. Duffy found himself reading the last word over and over. Death-death-death-death . . . .

I'm not afraid, he thought. *I'm terrified.*

The handwriting was irregular and shaky, as if someone were trying to write by holding the end of the pen. The 'o' was made with the connecting link going up like a camel's back, and the 'i' was separate from the following vowels. The handwriting was his. So was the greasy sweat on his brow.

After awhile he got up and opened the door of Anne's bedroom. Dark hair framed the white oval of her face; he knew without seeing her eyes that she was awake. "Anne . . . what are you doing?"

"Nothing. I was asleep."

"Why are you awake now?"

"I dreamed . . . that I was you. A long time ago. You were playing, no, fighting. With your brother. Over something your mother had given you."

"Was there anything about me in the present?"

"Just a feeling."

"What kind?"

"Of being very frightened. Are you?"

"I was. I'm still shaky."

"You want to get in bed with me, Alvin?"

A heavy scent reached his nose, a smell of musk that made his nostrils flare. He took a step into the room, and then stopped. "No, Anne. I'm going to have a drink and then go to bed."

Next morning during breakfast he showed her what he had written during his lapse the night before. She read it slowly, stirring a spoonful of cream into her oatmeal. Then she closed the notebook and handed it back to him.

"Does it tell you anything?"

"It tells me it has attitudes similar to Man's. There's an

undertone of arrogance which is totally human. And I'm thinking that if this thing has been around as long as it says, it should have left it's mark on the subconsciousness of Man. Like worm-tracks in fossilized stone. Since it preys on Man, the awareness would probably take the form of some basic, primeval fear. What are most people afraid of?"

"Well, commonly, the dark."

"Therefore, it is a creature of nocturnal habits. Judging from what you've told me, it's most active at night, so that fits. What else? People are repelled by slime. This may suggest that it was at one time, amphibious. People are afraid of . . . . "

"Spiders."

"Right. But why?"

She shuddered. "They're crawly."

"All right. Slimy and crawly. Likes the dark. Snails, frogs, toads . . . no, cancel the last two. They don't crawl. Maybe the damn thing slithers."

"Verne saw a blue light, with blackness around it."

"Hmmm. Did any of the others see anything?"

"If they did, they didn't tell me."

"Hmmm. Maybe we could get it to manifest itself. What were the conditions when Verne saw it?"

"Night-time. He was drunk and we had just finished making love."

"I see." His heartbeat quickened, hot blood rushed to his face and his ears started ringing. He forced himself to speak: "I think I would feel desire for you under any circumstances—but I must admit it's unusually strong at the moment. Is there any way of telling which is normal and which is a manifestation of the creature's urge to bring us together?"

"No." Her voice was like velvet around the words. "I feel it too."

The light of early morning shone through the window and touched the curve of her cheek, piercing the thin night-dress and silhouetting a breast. He could not believe she would harbor anything evil. But of course the creature would camouflage itself from its prey. It would hide behind dazzling beauty, like a hawk diving out of the sun.

He stood up suddenly. "Anne, I'm going out for a long

walk. I don't know . . . . " He stopped, realizing he wasn't even sure what he didn't know. "Maybe I'm not strong enough to help you. I'm going to think it over."

He walked until his hips ached. He climbed ridges until his thigh muscles would not lift the weight of his body. His belly ached with hunger, and he realized he'd been on the move for at least five hours. *Obsessive escape pattern,* he thought as he filled his pipe for the first time since leaving the chalet. He decided it would be simpler to make love to her and take the consequences. Well, more fun at least. The creature had already proved its ability to take control.

The return journey was twice as hard, since he carried the added burdens of fatigue and hunger. He got home just after sunset and jumped into the pool. He ran dripping into his bedroom and dried himself with a briskness that burned his skin. He felt strong, proud of his body's performance that day, confident of his ability to please her. He knotted the damp towel around his waist and pushed open the door of the living room.

She sat before the fireplace, her feet tucked under her. She wore red riding pants, soft leather boots, and a loosely-woven white sweater with nothing beneath it—that was obvious as she rose and walked toward him with the grace of a woman who is absolutely sure of her body and the gratification it can give. Her arms slid around his neck and he felt the soft pressure of her breasts and hips. "Alvin, I've decided to leave."

Her words were so contradictory to her actions that he was stunned. "Why?"

"You said it yourself. I need a stronger man."

Masculine pride rose up inside him. He thought she might be playing a refined version of the old rape-me game; he considered throwing off his towel and crushing her to the floor, ripping away her clothing with his teeth and taking her amid the tattered scraps.

She was smiling. "I would enjoy it, Duffy. But you would die afterward. I wouldn't enjoy that."

He swallowed a hard hot lump in his throat. "I'll risk it."

"It wouldn't be a risk. A dead certainty." She touched her lips lightly to his. "Goodbye Duffy. You've helped me. Now I know what sort of man to look for."

He watched her walk away and pick up a cowhide valise

that sat beside the door. "I hope you find him," said Duffy with a twist of bitterness. As the door clicked shut behind her, he said softly: "And may God have mercy on his soul."

It was several minutes before he remembered that she had a three-mile walk to the highway. He could at least give her a lift, and maybe persuade her to stay. He got in his car and drove down the twisting road, expecting at each turn to see her white sweater and red pants in the headlights. But no.

He drove all the way to the highway, checked the little restaurant at the intersection, and drove a mile each way on the highway. Nobody. He drove back to the chalet with the feeling that his heart had been torn from his chest.

He was brooding his way through the third Irish whiskey and water when the thought stabbed him like a knife: You're being controlled, Duffy. Where is the cold fire of ambition, the gimlet gleam of scientific curiosity, the ivory perfection of the intellect which permits nothing to obscure the truth? You have been seeded, Duffy. She has planted something in you and has stepped aside to wait until it grows. She will return.

"Ridiculous," he said to the fire.

Test it then. Try to leave.

"I don't want to leave."

You see?

"Even if she came back it would prove nothing—except that she wants me."

She loves you, Duffy. Like a rabbit loves lettuce.

"Shut up!" He swung his arm and shattered the squat little glass against the stone facing the fireplace. Cleaning up the mess gave him something to do. Afterward he made coffee and drank it while he paced the floor. Uncounted times he looked out of the window. Twice he walked out to the road and looked down it, teasing himself with the fantasy that she would return, wet and penitent. He would fix her bath and dry her with the towel, rubbing her cold white buttocks until they turned pink.

He went to bed, finally. When he awoke at dawn he was gratified to realize that he had slept. He looked into her bedroom and saw that nothing had been disturbed.

He spent the day with a buck-saw, cutting logs for his fireplace. He didn't care if she appeared with a knife aimed at his throat, he just wanted to see her. *God, is this normal?* That night he went to sleep while playing over the interviews he'd taped with her. He awoke in a cold dawn with the headphones humming in his ears.

Sometime during the afternoon it occurred to him that he was losing his sanity. He went to the phone and dialed the number of a girl who'd spent several weekends in the chalet. The sound of her voice brought a picture of Sally: tall, slim, blonde, so self-conscious about her large breasts and so energetic in lovemaking . . . . He hung up silently. She seemed unreal, a polished porcelain illusion. Anne was the only reality. She would not return, she had no reason because she had already eaten him from the inside: He was a grasshopper husk sitting on a dry stalk in autumn, a puffball which retains its shape though nothing but dry dust remains inside.

Once he realized that it was a simple matter of deciding on a method. He had no desire to cause a fuss, or leave behind a mess for somebody to clean up. He had everything he needed: Sleeping tablets. An electric alarm clock. Dynamite. He'd leave nothing behind for the morticians to paint, powder and perfume.

The timing device proved to be the most complicated. The printed circuits in his travel-clock made him swear in frustration, but he managed to rewire the alarm to send a spurt of electricity into a blasting cap. The resulting bang echoed up and down the valley for several minutes. *You ain't heard nothin' yet,* he thought. He had five dynamite sticks left from blasting out the pool. He made two slits in the stuffed leather armchair that sat before his fireplace, shoved three of the wax-papered cylinders into the seat, and the other two in the back. Testing the chair he found it lumpy, so he got up and wriggled the dynamite deep into the padding. Next he affixed the detonator caps, leaving the lead-in wire loose while he went for the pills and a glass of water.

Have I forgotten anything? he wondered as he settled himself in the chair. *Barbiturates here on the right hand side of the chair. Triple the lethal dose.* Within ten minutes he would be unconscious; in thirty minutes his body processes would slow to the point where nothing could revive him. The clock said nine-thirty. He set the alarm for ten o'clock and spliced in the wires leading to the dynamite.

He leaned back, took the water in one hand and the pills in another, and wondered if he were insane. He had no standard for measuring his own sanity, no place to stand in the swirling void. He laughed softly and tipped the pill bottle to his mouth. It went down like a handful of popcorn. He lifted the glass and swallowed three times, then tongued a recalcitrant pill out from behind his lower lip. The deed was done. He wiped his mouth and set the glass on the floor. The second hand crawled around the face of the clock. One minute. Two. Three. Time was slowing down. After five minutes he felt his limbs getting heavy; ten minutes, and he could see the clock only through the narrow slits of his eyelids.

A finger pushed down the alarm button. It was attached to a long, feminine hand. A familiar hand. With a gritty effort he raised his head and pushed out the word: "Anne . . . ."

Her beloved face was a mask of ivory. Her sweater was smudged and raveled, her pants were torn, and her hair was a bird's nest of twigs and dry leaves. Something had happened, but hers was not the most urgent problem. Why did his brain move so slowly? He had to find a way to tell her about the pills. The dynamite would not explode, but he needed stimulants, exercise, emetics, purgatives, stomach pump, hospital. His mouth felt stuffed with sawdust. "Anne . . . the pills . . . ."

"This isn't Anne," said a dry distant voice.

The sound raised his hair. He looked into her eyes and saw that the iris had been pushed out by the swelling pupil until only a hairline of green remained. The rest was a wet gleaming blackness which gave twin images of a sleepy looking man with rough blunt features seated in a high-backed leather chair.

"You . . . took over?" he asked.

A smile appeared on the face.

"What are . . . you?"

The smile spread slightly.

"What . . . are you going . . . to do?"

Delicately she lowered herself to the hassock and placed

one leg over the other. Then she folded her hands and looked into his eyes.

Duffy made one last gasping attempt. "You took me . . . where I was weakest. Trapped by my curiosity."

"Goodbye, Duffy."

The blackness in her eyes swelled up and swallowed his vision. His hearing quit, and for the first time in his life he knew the deafening roar of silence. His sense of touch left him. He became a thought suspended in hot darkness.

Then he felt the little nibblings.

EIGHT

THE woman sat on the hassock, hands folded in her lap. The man slumped in the leather armchair, head bent and eyelids half-closed. A casual observer might have assumed he was dozing, if his chest had not remained fallen and still.

Hours passed, while the hands moved slowly around the face of the clock on the coffee table. The man's body settled deeper into the chair as tendons and muscles relaxed their lifetime struggle against gravity. A human ear would have heard vague rustling sounds, like the whisper of dry grass in a breeze. The figure seemed to shrink, as the cells collapsed upon themselves.

Only the dead know death. The living know only that heart action stops and breathing ends. The brain ticks on until its activity falls below the threshold of man's detection. When does life end? Does it ever? Man devours the unknown with his science, chewing it into ever smaller pieces and defecating names and numbers and categories. But the Unknown remains.

Anne rose from the hassock, her joints stiff from inactivity. Duffy's alarm clock said five-twenty, and dawn was arriving in the east. She yawned and stretched, regarding the corpse in the chair with a sense of repleteness and satisfaction. It was good to be in control of her body again after three days. She re-set the alarm and pulled out the button. It took only a minute to gather up the tapes Duffy had made during the interviews, throw them into a suitcase with a change of clothing, and go out the door.

She'd gone only two hundred yards down the road when the entire mountain seemed to explode above her. She glanced back and saw fragments of redwood and stone billowing out like confetti flung from a window. Into the road ahead fell a smoking fragment of polished leather which she recognized as part of the hassock on which she'd been sitting. She stood still for a minute, listening to the echoes of the blast mingle with the crash and rattle of debris returning to earth. There was a moment of utter silence, followed by the hollow boom of a gas explosion. She gazed at the vortex of black smoke billowing upward and heard the crackle of flames. Duffy had prepared well. There would be nothing left to examine.

Twice she had to leave the road to avoid cars racing up the mountainside. On a bridge she stopped to throw the tapes down into the rushing white water. When she reached the highway she waited until a man left the restaurant and got into his car. "Going east?" she asked. He shifted his toothpick from one corner of his mouth to the other, and a smile pulled at his lips. "Sure, get in."

She rode with him to Amarillo and left him, sexually frustrated and unaware of how lucky he was to be that way. There she withdrew the savings she'd deposited five years before, and transferred the money and accrued interest to a checking account. The amount ran into six figures but she took no satisfaction in that; money was important only in that it gave her power and mobility. She needed both, to carry out the dual task which she now saw clearly for the first time: One, locate and destroy David Hall, the only mortal who knew her secret. Two, find a male of her species and mate with him. Presumably she would know how when the time came, just as humans and lower animals copulate by instinct. The years had been lonely, and no man had ever filled the gnawing emptiness she felt inside her.

Two days later, at nine in the morning, she stoppped her rented car outside the farmhouse which had once been her grandfather's. The name on the mailbox was Reardon. Other things had been changed too; a swing hung from the oak tree, chickens scratched around the front door, and the backyard was littered with junk autos. A husky, taffy-haired young man dropped his wrench and came forward. The grime of machinery seemed embedded in his skin; only his blue eyes were clean. His hostile look softened as he approached the car, changing finally to a friendly grin when he rested his forearms on the window frame.

"He died," he replied when she asked about Maynard Grosz. "I think it was three years ago, and the widow went to live with her daughter. I think the old lady died too, but I ain't sure. We make our payments to the bank. I dunno the address of the daughter, it's up in the city."

"There's a David Hall who owns the place across the valley. You know him?"

"Oh, the cripple?" He glanced at a short dark-haired woman who stood in the doorway and laughed in embarrassment. "Well, I just can't tell you much about him. We went over there once when we first moved here. The guy couldn't talk, just wrote notes. And the woman wouldn't come downstairs. It was . . . I dunno, we never went back. I guess they never went out, did they, Wanda?"

The dark-haired girl spoke in a small, shy voice. "They had the phone took out and the electric cut off and put up a steel gate at the head of their lane with a big old padlock on it." There was a hint of anger and hurt in her voice. "They wasn't much for neighboring, that's all I can say."

The man said: "Last summer a limb blowed off the maple tree and fell across the front steps. I noticed a couple months ago that it was still there. So I figure they moved away."

She thanked him and drove down the gravel road which dwindled to a dirt track and ended at a steel gate. She climbed over and walked down the weed-grown lane. The unpainted frame house had a two-story section in front and a gabled kitchen extending out the back. Noticing the rusted padlock on the door, she went around to the kitchen, smashed a window with a dry tree-limb, and climbed through. She felt as if she'd been transported a hundred years back in time. The kitchen fireplace nearly filled one wall, and a black iron cauldron hung above a pile of gray wood ashes. At one side of the room stood an antique dry-sink holding a white porcelain pitcher and bowl. Rough benches flanked a table made of hand-hewn logs. In one of the front rooms she found a spinning wheel with woolen thread wrapped around the spindle. In the seat of a bentwood rocker lay two carding brushes, with a sack of wool beside it. Upstairs she found a canopied four-poster bed. Rag carpets on the hardwood floor. In a dresser drawer were sunbonnets of a style she remembered from pictures of the Civil War era, woolen stockings and, wonder of wonders, a pair of black bloomers with elastic at the knees. In the other room stood a steel cot, a wheel-chair folded against the wall, a workbench with wood-carving tools racked above it.

She descended the stairs and went out back. An old barn had collapsed like an overloaded burro, its walls splayed out and its roof dropped into the center. She walked around it and found an overgrown path leading to an apple orchard. Broken limbs littered the ground; a beehive had blown over and dried combs were scattered everywhere.

The hollyhocks drew her attention to the grave. They grew six feet high along the fence, old-fashioned pink and purple cups clustered around a central spike. The wooden marker was four feet high, carved of soft pine and apparently treated with some preservative chemical. An angel in bas-relief spread her wings over letters cut deeply into the wood:

NORA GATES
who lived another life as
MARGARET TUTTLE
1846-1974

So David had come back to the woman from the fort, and had brought her here to die. And what had he learned from her? It would be helpful to find out, before she did what was necessary.

The woman in the little post office confirmed that David Hall had indeed left the county. "Stopped all his mail, no forwarding address. Don't know what happens to his government checks. He used to have 'em sent care of this girl up in the city. Janet Blythe. I remember the name because my husband's sister married a man named Blythe, of Welsh extraction, no relation though far as I know."

Janet, my old girlhood chum. Anne felt the memories

crowd in as she drove north toward the city. Skipping rope together, holding hands around the campfire, saving money together to buy a new Dylan album . . . . Strange to think that only seven years had passed since she'd seen Janet. Anne wondered if she needed to disguise herself. A glance in the rear-view mirror told her she was fairly safe. Her red-brown hair had darkened to a near-sooty black. The green eyes gave back a level stare that seemed ageless. She was no longer Anne; too much of what had happened was written in her face, like an invisible script which lay just beneath the surface of her skin.

The population of the lake had changed; few of the names Anne remembered as a child were still there. Nobody clung very long near the top of the ladder; they either moved up, or slid down. Anne could tell, as she drove slowly past her old home, that her mother had slid. The paint around the windows had a faded look, the yard was shaggy and the hedges unclipped, one of the concrete urns beside the driveway had been knocked over and broken, so long ago that weeds grew in the spilled dirt.

Anne drove around the lake and parked in front of Janet's house. As she went up the familiar sidewalk, the spaniel she had known as a roly-poly puppy ran around the house yapping. It saw her and skidded to a stop, then backed away with a low muttering growl. Anne paid no attention, for dogs always reacted to her in that manner.

Janet opened the door and nodded with the polite reserve of someone greeting a respectable-looking but unknown caller. A solid chunky girl with a broad face and dark-blonde hair, Janet could in no way have made herself beautiful and she had the intelligence not to try. Freckles still sprayed across her nose, and the teeth had never quite closed up in front, but she managed to project a wholesome, pleasant personality.

Anne said: "I'm looking for David Hall. I was told you might know where I could find him."

"No . . . . " Janet frowned and pinched her chin. "You know David?"

"I met him years ago."

"Well he's gone. He said he wouldn't be back. Ever." She tilted her head and looked at Anne curiously. "You know he had a kidney ailment and didn't expect to live."

"I know. I thought he might have left a message."

The girl glanced over her shoulder, then stepped out and closed the door. Motioning with her hand, she went around the house and into the backyard. There was the old gazebo, still shrouded in climbing roses, where she and Janet had spent many long summer afternoons. Janet leaned against the low railing and waited until Anne sat down in the glider which hung from two chains.

"You know there used to be this girl who lived across the lake, Anne was her name. My very best friend when I was a girl, but she ran away. I'm very close to her brother right now. We have an apartment downtown. Billy goes to engineering school; I happen to be home today because my mother is sick. We'll get married if his family situation ever clears up."

"I see." Anne found the picture of Billy and Janet mildly interesting, but totally unsurprising. "What family situation?"

"There's this man living with his mother. Just an absolute . . . bum. Oh, I suppose he has lovable qualities, but I've never been able to see them. I never go over there any more because he's always trying to make out with me. I don't know why he picks on me, because he's the official stud of Lake Rothermere. God's gift to lonely housewives. He spent all her insurance money on speedboats and racing cars, then he took off. Billy's mother was broke for awhile, then Anne started sending money home, and he came back. She just signs the checks over to him and he spends the money. There's a second mortgage on the house but he never pays it, and Billy never gets any money. I have to work at Daddy's lab to help Billy through engineering school, he's carrying such a heavy load . . . . "

"Yes," said Anne. "You were telling me about David . . . . "

"Oh yes. Well I got him a job in Daddy's lab, not that it was charity, because David was a good chemist. He and I got pretty close—not in a romantic sense, but we talked about life and death and what's happening in the world. He'd gone to see Billy's sister, Anne, and she'd gotten into some strange things which he'd never explain. He just thought she'd be back, or maybe she'd send somebody. He left a letter for whoever it might be . . . . "

The girl was waiting, her head tilted to one side. "I'll see that she gets it," said Anne.

Janet nodded. "I had that feeling, when I saw you at the door." She climbed up on the railing and ran her hand under the eaves. *I could have found it myself,* thought Anne. *That's where we hid the pornographic magazine I swiped from Billy.* The memory was bittersweet. Things past and gone and never-to-return, and did she really care? Janet was the girl she herself might have been; the heavy thighs, visible as the girl stretched her arms upward, showed nicks where she'd cut herself shaving. No, it was a pointless excursion into nostalgia. Even if she wanted to, she could never again pass through the eye of that particular needle.

Janet jumped down holding a thickly padded envelope. "David wanted me to be sure only Anne would read the letter. He gave me a question to ask before handing it over: Who owned the yacht which took you out of Houston?"

"Haverill," said Anne.

Janet held out the envelope in trembling fingers. "You're Anne. Really Anne."

"Yes. Don't tell anybody."

"But . . . . " The girl's lips quivered, and her eyes filled with tears. "What happened to you? You look different, older . . . and beautiful!"

"The price is tremendous. Be happy with what you've got. Goodbye." She took the girl's trembling hand in hers, but Janet stepped up and gave her a little-girl kiss on the cheek that made Anne feel a hundred years old.

"Goodbye . . . sister."

Anne drove to a drive-in, ordered a malt, and tore off the end of the envelope:

> Dear Anne: Men of the Hall family tend to small stature, but beneath the puny exterior strides a monumental ego. I refused to die in Houston, though it was close. A cleaning lady found me and called an ambulance. The hospital experience is best forgotten; they ran new blood through me like rinse through a bundle of dirty laundry, and after eight months pronounced me clean, with a life-expectancy of four years—two less than before. At the club I learned that you'd gone with Haverill on his

yacht, which was last seen leaving Panama destined for the Fiji Islands. Wreckage was found which indicated an explosion and fire aboard the ship; two crewmen were picked up and reported that Haverill had gone berserk and started killing the crew. You know what happened better than I. My assumption was that you worked your magic on Haverill and brought his timely death. I weep not. Remembering that you survived a mortal bayonet wound, I did not, as the authorities did, discount you as dead.

I returned here to keep in touch with your mother and await your return. Meanwhile I kept up my visits with Margaret in the hospital. My reputation was good, and since the unfortunate woman grew fond of me, I had her released to my care. But she was confused by the city and terrified of machinery, so I took her back to the farm and created an environment in which she felt at ease. She was aging at least a year every month. It seems that when the creature left her it also withdrew the support it had been giving her system. She died after three years, looking at least seventy. Though her memory never returned, she had brief remissions of her amnesia so that I was able to piece together a vague picture of the creature's habits. By now you may have learned all this, but in case you haven't you may find it helpful.

Bear in mind that Margaret was not basically intelligent; in a normal lifetime she would have married a farmer and borne his children and done his laundry and died without ever considering the why of existence. She reacted to the creature in terms of witchcraft. She said a spell had been laid on her by a squaw whom Margaret had seen copulating with a bear in the woods. (This was probably true, as you will see later.) Apparently the creature transferred itself from the squaw to Margaret. To explain how this happened, I must abandon poor Margaret's witchcraft analogy and proceed in scientific terms.

Briefly, the X-parasites (the name I have assigned the creature) come in two sexes. Whether this is natural or a convenience to fit the earth-scheme of ecology I do not know. They begin life as amoebalike creatures which resemble black egg-yolks without shells—or would, if they were visible. (Margaret said they could be seen only by those who had the Evil Eye, by which I think she meant extra-sensory perception.) Lacking protection, the creatures must find a host within five to eight hours or die. The sex of the organisms they inhabit first determines their own sex for all the centuries of their lives. While they can transfer from one host to another—i.e., from an aging female to a young one—they can't switch from a female to a male, or vice versa. Other differences between the sexes are unclear to me. I imagine the creatures themselves see a difference, but to us it's like trying to ascertain the sex of a jelly fish. They mate every seven years, and one ameobalike offspring results. This ameoba seeks to inhabit the highest animal form around. If there are no humans in the vicinity, it will inhabit an animal and remain there until it finds a higher life-form, then it will switch. Switching is accomplished when the X-parasite causes the desired host to kill the current host. Thus if an inhabited rabbit is shot by a man, the X-parasite uses death-agony force to propel itself into the man. (The New World seems to have been overrun with the creatures before the coming of the white man. Witness the Indian belief that hunters took on the spirits of the animals they killed. Witness the Mayan and Aztec priests, who ate the victims of sacrifices in order to acquire their souls.)

My information on the creature's feeding habits is sketchy. Its diet seems to be some kind of life-force which human scientists have not yet managed to isolate. It usually makes contact during intercourse, extruding a sort of digestive mechanism which enters the body of the victim. At such times the creature is vulnerable, since its brain center occupies the body which is being eaten. Thus if a third party happens by, the X-parasite must leave its meal and jump—into darkness, so to speak, since it is temporarily cut off from its sensory apparatus. Often it finds its way into the third party. This is how Margaret acquired her Nemesis, and probably this is how she lost it. I judge that she seduced your father, and that you happened along and . . . .

But these memories may be painful.

The thing you saw in the underground room (I heard

about it from your brother Bill) was one of Margaret's offspring in its amoebic state. Instinctively it sought to hide in the nearest available organism—which happened to be a lizard. Your brother killed the lizard before the X-parasite was able to hook into the vital centers. Thus it was trapped in a dying body, unable to tap the energy it needed. I assume that it died.

You, meanwhile, were taken over by Margaret's creature. Naturally it was hungry; it needed food energy in order to rebuild your body into a shape more attractive to the opposite sex, which in turn would make it easier to feed itself. Probably it took shape from your own mental picture of how an ideal woman should look. When your ideal changed, you would change to fit it. Thus you would adapt to a new situation with the speed of a chameleon; i.e., if you were suddenly transported to the Arctic, you might sprout fur, or grow a layer of blubber under your skin.

I was unable to learn from Margaret just how the creatures breed, or how they find each other during the season of rut. She was shy, in a way you cannot imagine unless you're familiar with the Victorian mentality. She claimed total amnesia on the subject (which I doubt) though she remembers that she made love (in human fashion) with one man a number of times. But she also remembers a wolf, and a horse. She insists that it took place on a physical level. My mind boggles—but I admit the possibility.

In any case, Margaret was bred by a male member of the X-parasite species during the few days preceding your visit to the fort. On the chance that the host was human, I have taken the names of all men who signed the visitors' book. I am going now—having buried poor Margaret—and will check them out. If one is the host, I shall watch for a chance to capture his creature. The ethical questions are legion, but life as host to an X-parasite seems better to me than no life at all.

I leave this letter with Janet, since I have been unable to penetrate the manifold cloak of your anonymity. The bank which sends your mother checks receives instructions from an anonymous law firm which is paid by a trust fund established by an unknown individual . . . .

Anyway I haven't time to find you now. Less than a year remains of the span my doctors alloted to me. If my search is successful, I will find you. If not . . . well, life is short at best, and I hope you can use the information herein. Love, David.

The letter was two years old. If the doctors were right, then David was dead. Some vestige of human conscience told her she should feel sorry for him. But if he was dead, then he no longer existed, so whom should she mourn? The David that existed yesterday? Yesterday did not exist either, so . . . .

There was nothing to feel sorry for.

She set fire to the letter and turned it while the flames consumed all but one corner. Then she tossed it out on the gravel and honked her horn for the carhop. A man pulled into the space beside her and smiled. She admired the muscular arm which rested on the window—but he wore glasses and his teeth were not the best.

The best was what she had to find, for only the most outstanding males were likely to harbor the mate she sought. Such a man would not go out and prowl for women; he'd just sit back and make his choice, and who would resist him? But he'd have to keep moving, or else operate from concealment, otherwise the carcasses of his kill would clog his doorway.

She paid the ticket and started driving west.

NINE

THE afternoon was hot. The air was still, except when a dust-devil whirled through the speedway, skipping off through the sagebrush beyond the chain-link fence. Anne dabbed her forehead with a napkin and gazed up at the poster. The motorcyclist looked cool as he floated above the long row of automobiles. His long blond hair streamed out behind his head, his white teeth showed in a perfect smile, and his eyes danced with the manic laughter of one who defies death for his daily bread.

She paid the price and went in. Several other women sat alone, unnoticed among the couples, family groups, and amorphic clumps of adolescent young who occupied the rough planks of the bleachers. Anne watched the boy circle the ramps on his red-and-blue motorcycle with white streamers fluttering out behind the handlebars. She felt the sexual excitement of the other women; they wanted to share the boy's death, they wanted his last orgasm, the last cupful of his manhood. They wanted him to die, then they wanted to weep for him. It was all very low-level, human.

But she wasn't sure about the rider. Watching him roar up the ramp, his pipes ripping the air in a great blast of sound, she pitied his soft human flesh. Her heart soared as he shot off the ramp. He seemed suspended above the shining domes of the cars; Anne's eyes darted ahead to the opposite ramp, lining up its slope with the angle of his wheels, watching for a too-sudden drop which would smash him against the ramp like a bug on a windshield. But the angle was right. He touched down with a screech of rubber and a deep sigh of shock-absorbers. As he circled the ramps, she joined the crowd streaming down onto the track. He looked thinner close up, harried and restless, with a sour twist to his mouth. He signed a few autographs and then tossed his pen to a bouquet of clutching hands, stretching his neck to look over the crowd. His eyes met hers and he nodded his head. The peremptory male summons. Anne smiled to herself and went forward. It was the way *she* would have done it, if she'd been him.

"What's your name?"

"Anne."

"Well Anne, you stand back there smiling and you don't want an autograph. You wanta ride on my bike? A piece of my uniform? What?"

She understood him then. He wanted shelter from the cold wind blowing through his soul. He sought her as a spot of warmth on the glacier of life. He was driven by fear, blinking, turning and shifting as he tried to look sideways into the eyes of death. A month ago she would have wasted a night, but she had tested many like him, and all had died, and her heart was no longer in it.

"None of those things," she said, and walked away.

She had the sense of being followed as she drove out of the parking lot. On the highway, she kept getting vague glimpses of her car's rear bumper and license plates—as seen through other eyes. But she couldn't pick the follower out of the line of cars behind her. There seemed to be no threat involved, only a tentative, hidden purpose.

Ten miles later the pursuer was still behind her. She pulled into a restaurant and ordered a meal of steak and eggs. She didn't turn when the door opened, but she felt him scan the house and then approach the seat she'd left vacant beside her. As he sat down, her nose caught the smell of booze and expensive cigars. The hand that reached for the menu was long and well-tended, with manicured nails and a diamond ring glittering on the little finger.

"I like the way you eat," he said, "like a perfect animal."

She looked at him. His suit was the latest fashion, his hair was styled long and full on the sides. His capped teeth gleamed beneath a silky blond moustache. His face sloped back suddenly from the sharp edge of nose and chin, giving him a look of canine ferocity. She recognized him as a predator of a different class than herself—one who liked to run in a pack, who adopts the manner of civilized man, clothes the wolf-body in fine threads and hides his fangs in the brilliance of his smile. But the eyes gave him away. Hard brilliant and blue, they sat deeply in their sockets and observed the herd, waiting for the first sign of weakness to dart in and pull down a victim.

Anne dumped cream in her coffee, stirred it once, and lifted it to her lips. "Conducting a survey of eating habits, are you?"

She let her eyes bore into his. He made quick flickering glances right and left, then he seemed to pull back into himself. His voice held a note of injury: "I didn't mean it in a disparaging sense."

Saying nothing, she rose and paid her bill, then walked out. Beside her rented Chrysler was parked a long gray luxury automobile of some Italian make. He came out and leaned against it with his hands thrust deeply into his pockets, watching her get into her car.

"Would you like to come with me?"

She shook her head. "No chance."

Smiling like a man with a secret, he withdrew his hand from his pocket and unfolded a banknote with the number "100" at each corner. Creasing it with his index finger like a cigarette paper, he thrust it through her car window. Anne ignited her cigarette lighter and held it under the bill. She watched his eyes as the smoke curled up and the flame ate back toward his finger. He jerked back his hand and his eyes wrinkled with pain. Anne reached for her key.

"Wait, please. Tell me what you want."

"What makes you think I want anything?"

"I saw you at the motorcycle show. You were looking."

"Yes. For a man who isn't afraid of death." She smiled and started her engine. "You don't qualify."

He waited until she had backed out of the parking space and shifted to forward gear, then he called: "I know one who does!"

She drove on down the road a couple of miles before she began to consider it seriously. Her initial reaction had lumped him with a great mass of free loading males, beach boys and bellhops, hairdressers and gigolos, all those who carry their manhood like a product to be sold, traded, cashed in, exchanged for kind words, free meals and lodging. Such men did not usually pursue her, preferring the easier mark. Yet she saw in her rear-view mirror that the gray car was a quarter-mile behind her, three cars back. She pulled onto a side road and stopped. A minute later he pulled up beside her and grinned across the space between them.

"What hooked you? My suave technique?"

"I want to know about the man who isn't afraid of death."

He climbed out and sauntered over, twirling his keys on his finger. "He's done everything. Raced cars in the mountains of Italy, lived for weeks in a diving bell. He's been a skydiver too, a polo star, tennis champion. Here." He took out a folder of plastic photo envelopes. Anne flipped through pictures of a young blond man wearing flowers, holding loving cups, receiving kisses from movie stars, shaking hands . . . and in each photo his face wore exactly the same smile, showed exactly the same number of shining white teeth. She studied a picture of him in the baggy white trousers and black belt of a karate expert, and asked: "What does he do for a living?"

The man laughed. "Mr. Van is worth about a quarter of a billion dollars. He does what he likes."

"Mr. Van?"

"Dirk Van Diemann."

The name was not familiar to Anne—but then she'd never flown in the circles of the ultra-rich, nor did she read the social columns where their activities were so slavishly reported. "Is this your job, finding women for him?"

His chin came up slightly. "I'm his lawyer."

"And Dirk Van Diemann can afford to hire a lawyer as his pimp, correct?"

His lips thinned out in a mackerel smile. "When the price runs to four figures, words like pimping and whoring seem unnecessarily crude, wouldn't you say?"

"Four figures?" She smiled, took her key out of the switch, and held it out to him. "I have a suitcase in back. Would you get it?"

"What about your car?"

"They'll discover it sooner or later. And the rental agency has another key."

The lawyer's name was Joe Carrick. He lived twenty miles away in a desert condominium built around a glittering blue lake. His apartment was deluxe, with a white-carpeted stairway spiraling up to a balcony which overlooked the living room. He carried her bag up to one of the bedrooms and suggested she might like to bathe and change. His manner had turned brusque, and she began to feel like a piece of baggage.

"When do I meet Dirk?"

"I'll call him now," he said, and went out.

In the bathroom she found a long black tub fitted with gold faucets. The vanity alcove and douching stool revealed that it had been designed for women, or for men with European habits. She turned the faucets, then undressed and stepped into the tub. The water was exactly the right warmth, imbued with a minty fragrance. Mirrors were placed so that she could watch herself in the tub. Her ivory shoulders gleamed, her breasts were buoyed up into a fertile fullness. She let the spreading warmth soothe her body and rested the back of her neck on the cool tiles.

The door opened, and Carrick came in with two frosted, tinkling glasses. Placing one on the rim of the tub, he sat down on the low padded bench beside it. "Mr. Van will see you tonight."

Anne lifted her glass and sipped the cool Vodka and lemon. "I'll think about it."

Carrick shook his head. "Sorry, Anne. The coy scene won't work with Mr. Van. At eight o'clock you go with me to the club where he'll be. At midnight I pick you up and bring you back here. If you don't want to do it that way—" He jerked his thumb over his shoulder like an umpire.

"What's the name of the club?"

"Huh-uh. Can't tell you."

"I'd like to make a phone call. There's no phone in my room."

He shook his head again. "No phone calls."

"Suppose I walked out right now?"

He shrugged. "Suit yourself. I told him you burned the century-note. He laughed. 'Give her five thousand,' he said. So if you want to throw it down the drain . . . . "

She thought about it, sipping the drink. Money would mean little to the man she was looking for. Assuming that this was the way Van Diemann kept his creature fed, there would be no actual expense, since he could lift the money off the bodies later.

"I know it seems strange," Carrick was saying. "But Mr. Van gets a lot of trouble from little girls who smell big money. It's there—but the reason it's there is that Mr. Van can't be taken by cheap tricks like calling a husband or dragging in a baby nine months from now."

"I understand." Anne stepped out of the tub, letting the water run off her body and soak into the thick shag rug. She took a towel from the rack and tossed it to the lawyer. "Make yourself useful, Carrick."

She felt the tremor in his hands as he rubbed her back. He started to give back the towel, but she said, "You're doing fine." She sat down on the padded bench and waited until Carrick knelt before her, then she lifted her foot and rested it on his knee. "Tell me about the Van Diemanns. How did they make their fortune?"

"Well . . . Mr. Van's great-great-grandfather started it when he made a diamond strike in South Africa. Then his great-grandfather went to California to raise cattle, and found gold instead. His grandfather struck oil in Sumatra while he was clearing land to raise pepper trees. His father hit uranium in Utah. Dirk hasn't made his hundred million yet—but he will."

Anne closed her eyes and leaned back as his toweling progressed up her thighs toward her torso. "How is it that nobody ever hears about the Van Diemann fortune?"

"It's pretty well scattered over the world, for one thing. And the Van Diemann males don't show themselves in public."

"Are there any Van Diemann females?"

He shrugged. "I guess they have wives. But as far as offspring—there's only been one male heir per generation. That's a break, you know—keeps the fortune from splitting up."

Yes, thought Anne, but it would be the same if only one man existed through all those generations. She felt a growing anticipation of the meeting to come. Lifting her foot, she pressed it against the lawyer's groin and wriggled her toes. "When do you get your break, Carrick? After midnight?"

He lifted his eyes in a startled look, then turned away with a vague, non-committal shrug. "If you want to, sure. But nobody ever wants to—afterwards."

Which could mean anything, thought Anne, including the fact that most girls would be deathly ill by then . . . .

The club was reached by a tortuous gravel drive which wound upward through a juniper forest. Carrick stopped the car at a steel gate made of plates riveted to a frame. He set his brake, got out, and inserted a key into a lock on the left gatepost. The steel panels swung open, then closed again after they were through. The road surface had changed to asphalt. She saw the club—it looked like a five-story A-frame backed against a red sandstone cliff. As they passed a swimming pool, a platinum-haired girl in a topless suit bounced once on the board and arched outward. Carrick drove around behind the club and stopped without switching off the engine. He pointed to a half-dozen chalets which studded the cliff. "Number two. Pick you up at midnight." He handed her a long white envelope. "It's all there, no holdout. Mr. Van often gives a generous bonus, so I would advise—"

"Stick to your own specialty, Carrick." She shoved the envelope in her purse and got out, feeling giddy as a girl on her first date. Impulsively she reached through the window and pinched Carrick's cheek. "See you at midnight. Don't turn into a mouse."

He drove off without smiling. As she climbed the steps to number two, Anne decided he was dreading the job of disposing of her body afterward. Best thing for him to do would be to haul her back to her car and prop her behind the wheel. Even if he'd been seen with her, there'd be nothing to indicate she hadn't died a natural death.

But I won't be dead, she thought. *Funny, I never considered how it felt from this end.*

She knocked and waited. The door opened and a voice said, "Come in." For a moment she didn't move. She stood and gazed at the chiseled perfection of his face, the jutting chin, the long straight nise, the long-lashed brown eyes. His hair made her think of butter and honey. From some distant dream-time of her childhood came the thought of

God, and what would happen if He should decide to make a perfect man.

Then why, she wondered, do I feel such an aching letdown?

He was incredibly polished. He took her purse with artful ease, held her chair at a table set for two. He gave her a cigarette and lit it, then sat down with his elbows resting on the table, looking over his folded hands.

"Your name is Anne?"

"Yes."

"What do you want, Anne?"

Something inside her curled away from his eyes. Anne felt a sudden, almost frightening sense of revulsion. *I never thought it would be like this. My God. He's different, he's not afraid of anything.*

And yet she wanted to pick up the serrated steak knife beside her plate and plunge it into her chest. Why? She didn't know, she'd never felt such a confusing mixture of emotions. She looked down at her hands, and decided there was nothing wrong with letting her confusion show.

"It's not for me to say, Dirk. You paid for me; I suppose you had in mind to use me as a woman."

"*Are* you a woman?"

Again, the twisting, curling revulsion inside her. He knows . . . or does he?

"Of course I'm a woman."

"Let's see it."

"What?"

He fluttered his fingers. "The parts that prove you're a woman. Display them."

She felt again the terrible, frightening urge to slash and kill. You perfect son-of-a-bitch. You conceited Adonis. You smug, self-assured sack of shit.

She stood up, unfastened the zipper in the side of her dress, and undid the snap in back. She wore nothing beneath it, so when the fabric fell to the floor she stood naked before him. He watched with a faintly bored expression, then got up from the table and stood in front of her.

His hand shot out, and the heel of his palm smacked her precisely between her breasts. She staggered, tripped, and sprawled backward onto a thick carpet.

She saw no emotion on his face as he looked down at her; he seemed to be measuring the precise distance between her breasts, the exact depth of her navel, the circumference of her thighs. It was a calculating look that left out any recognition of her as a woman.

"All right, Anne. We'll eat now."

As he walked away in steady even paces, she knew how it would feel to enjoy killing a man.

The food was hot, prepared and waiting on an electric hotplate set in the center of the table. Mock turtle soup; a salad of cucumbers, lettuce, green peppers; fresh water trout, golden-browned; and thick filet that peeled away from her knife like sod from a plow. The silver was so heavy her wrists ached from handling it; it was decorated with a monogram D-D worked into a serpent scroll which wound around the pen. No, it wasn't a serpent....

"Squid," he said, watching her across the table. "Giant squid. They live thousands of feet beneath the surface of the ocean. You never see them alive, since they explode in the upper ocean."

"And your family took it as an emblem?"

He nodded. "One of my . . . ancestors was a whaler. They used to get them out of the stomachs of the cachalot—sperm whale."

Silence. Anne found herself totally without appetite for the first time in her life. Her mouth was dry of saliva. Fear? Not exactly fear, just a tremendous uncertainty about the man across the table. She watched him take the wine from a silver bucket and come around the table to fill her goblet. She had a feeling that he never actually thought about anything, but merely waited until the time for action and then took the appropriate step. It occurred to her, as she watched him return to his chair, that generations of subservience to the creature had shriveled his humanity to a desicated remnant.

"I'm trying to see you as a boy, Dirk." She sat with her chin resting on her hands. "I suppose you caught frogs, snakes, insects, swam and went boating, things like that."

"We collected insects, killed them with chloroform, and stuck them on a board." He gazed steadily into her eyes, while his white teeth chewed the steak into a gray bloodless pulp.

"I see." She coughed and shifted her feet. "Did you enjoy it?"

"Only when we ran out of chloroform."

She glanced down, noticing his tanned hands resting on the table, golden hairs sprouting in precise squares behind each knuckle. She recalled that he'd lit her cigarette with his left hand, and eaten with his right. Ambidextrous, of course. His creature had done too well. She thought of her own too-wide mouth, the mole on her hip, the awkwardness of her left hand compared to her right. Perhaps there were personality differences between creatures. Possibly she and Van Diemann were incompatible to the core. All she knew was that she had no desire to mate with him on any level.

"My purse, please. I'm leaving."

He nodded and stood up, dabbing his lips. He got her purse from a wardrobe closet, then went to the door and opened it. "You may keep the money."

At that point her rage and frustration boiled over. She took out the envelope, ripped it down the center, and flung the two halves in his face. As he brushed away the tattered green squares, a smile played around his lips. He tilted his head and looked at her. "Feel better now?"

She felt the hot flush drain away from her face, leaving her cool and relaxed. "Why yes."

"Good. Then we can go." He pressed a button on the wall. "My car, please."

"Wait," said Anne. "Where are we going?"

"To see the man you came to see."

"You're not Van Diemann?"

"A paradoxical question. I *am* Van Diemann, when there is a need for someone to make a public appearance."

Anne felt a curious flooding of relief. His face was the same as the one in the photos Carrick had showed her. All of which had meant nothing, stacked up against her instinctive knowledge that this man had nothing to offer her. The real test was yet to come, though, and all of David's conclusions, and all of Duffy's theories, might still prove to be totally false.

"I'm wondering now," she said, "If there is such a man as Dirk Van Diemann."

He smiled and touched the small of her back with his hand. "There's the car now. You'll see him soon enough."

But it wasn't soon. By mid-afternoon of the following day they were still driving. Anne let her eyes rove the desert waste while her right hand stroked the white enamel of the door. New Ferrari, the most expensive model. She felt annoyed at the gray dust which curved up behind the car like breaking surf. She felt it sifting down on her forearms, gathering in the whorls of her ears, coating each hair. She'd have to wash it tonight before she—before *they* went to bed. Or whatever they did.

"What if I hadn't reacted last night?" She turned to the man behind the wheel. "You'd have turned me out at midnight without telling me the difference, wouldn't you?"

"That's correct."

"That's good." She thought about it and smiled. It was an effective screening system, first Carrick and then this guy, who'd told her to call him Webb. That's the way she'd have to set it up herself eventually, she decided. After a couple hundred years, you'd tend to get easily bored.

Like now. For three hours, ever since crossing the border into Mexico, they'd been jolting through a wasteland of slate-colored ridges and canyons and senseless heaps of beige rock. It was like a vast mine tailing overlaid by thornbrush and cactus. Every plant bristled with needles pointing directly at her. She counted eight lizards, four jack rabbits, two cottontails, two rattlesnakes and one horned toad before she tired of the game.

"Does he live alone on the estate?" she asked.

"There are servants," he said.

Into her mind came visions of a white-coated Filipino serving frosted drinks, a Mexican gardener touching his sombrero respectfully, a slim mulatto girl holding a towel as Anne stepped out of a sunken tub. Ah, the bath. She would soak for an hour . . . .

The car topped a ridge, and despite herself she felt joy rise inside her breast. "Oh! Stop!"

She was so entranced by the great sprawl of masonry that she didn't feel the car halt. The house could have been called a castle, if its style had not been so anomalous, fitting no time and no place, but creating its own atmosphere.

The tile roofs caught the reddening rays of the sun and in some areas glowed like hot coals, and in others turned a sullen black-red. Below them the walls, once whitewashed, were streaked with gray where the plaster had peeled away from the adobe. Vines rose from the ground like green surf, and the bougainvillea was a red flame crawling along the gallery. Pointed arches made her think of Arabian nights, but the front of the house was Grecian, with pillars and stone steps and a mosaic walkway leading down to a stone arch with a wrought-iron gate. The lawn was a sparkling emerald set in the slate stone of the desert.

"Lovely," she said, looking over at Webb. Without expression he put the car in gear and started down the slope. As he crossed a clear stream, she felt the coolness rise to her face. She thought how pleasant it would be to wade among the rocks and pick the watercress which matted the surface. The road changed from gravel to paving blocks, skirting an eight-foot stone wall which ran along the ridge behind the house. A studded wooden gate swung open an instant before the car's bumper touched it; the car rolled into a cobbled courtyard shaded by pepper trees. Turning, Anne saw a man bar the gates and walk toward her. He wore baggy linen pants and a leather vest. He set each sandaled foot directly before the other in the manner of an Indian; his eyes were like black cherries and his face was walnut, with a hatchet chin triangulating up to a broad Mayan forehead.

"Go with him," said Webb. "He'll take you to your room. You'll want to freshen up before you meet Mr. Van."

She climbed out of the car and said, *"Buenas tardes,"* but the Indian only turned and walked toward the house. She followed him, recalling that Webb had not spoken to him, nor had he spoken to Webb. A strange, unfriendly atmosphere.

When she saw her room, her breath left her again. Paneled walls of white, inlaid with golden scrolls. A tapestry covered one wall, definitely a Fragonard, with an impossibly sweet nude girl sitting with a fully clothed man in a jewel-like garden. The fireplace was fronted by blue porcelain, garnished with delicate nymphs and shepherds.

Hearing a sound from the bathroom, Anne went in and

saw a dark woman in a brown, sacklike dress bending over an ancient bathtub. It was an elaborate vessel standing eight inches off the floor on claw feet, its white enamel yellowed with age, and its gilt scrolls darkened by the years.

The woman straightened, wiping her hands on her dress and regarding Anne with a complete absence of expression. Anne smiled and tried her Spanish again: *"Me llamo Ana. Y usted?"*

The woman did nothing; her eyes gave no evidence that she was even trying to understand.

"You speak English?" asked Anne. *"Parlez vous francais? Sprechen sie Deutsch? Govoreetye Porusski?"*

Each question was followed by silence. The woman stood like a wall. At last Anne made a motion of dismissal, and the woman walked past her and left the room.

Anne undressed and stepped into the tub. The water was too cold. She twisted the hot water tap and listened to the trickle from distant pipes draw nearer until it coughed and gurgled into the tub. She leaned back into the soothing warmth and yawned.

A starter whirred, an engine coughed. She jumped out of the tub, seized a large mauve bath towel and ran barefoot onto the lawn. The Ferrari was disappearing over the far ridge; behind it rattled a dusty blue pickup which trailed a Spencerian scroll of gray dust. The sun blazed red on a distant mesa; the desert lay shadowless in the growing dusk. It was like a moon landscape, lonely and frightening.

She saw a man standing motionless near the front gate. Loneliness drew her to him, she felt grateful to him simply for being human, and being there. The cropped grass tickled the soles of her feet as she approached. When she was six feet away, he spoke, and she knew he'd been aware of her presence all the time.

"I sent them away, Anne. I thought it would be nice to be alone after all these years."

She stopped, frozen. *After all these years* . . . . The implication was that he knew her, yet she did not recognize the vibrant mellow tone of his voice. The breadth of his shoulders was startling, the neat taper of his back made her arms ache to hold him. The neck sloped up to small ears, and his hair—it seemed to be gold, or black—hung around his head in springy ringlets which teased her with the desire to run it through her fingers. The angle of his head denied her a glimpse of his features, but she could see his firm jaw, and the regular curve of his cheekbone. He was no monster, this was obvious. Why should she be afraid?

"Why indeed?" he said, and she realized he was reading her mind. It was frustrating to have the game turned on her that way—for his own mind was totally opaque to her.

She took a step closer, holding the towel above her breasts. At that moment he turned, smiling. His hand came out like a striking cobra and jerked the towel from her body. She stood naked, forgetting even to hold her breasts erect. She became aware that her body, half bent in concealmeant, had gradually evolved into an attitude of feminine submission. She found the pose restful, and hated herself for enjoying it. A thought came into her mind like a shadow from antiquity: *I am yours, my Lord. Do what you will.*

And he did, seizing her in his arms and drawing her to him in a kiss which reduced her muscles to water. His mouth drew the strength from her body; she felt her knees sag against his, then his arm went around her waist and his finger lifted her chin. "You know me now?"

The gray eyes, crinkled with amusement, the shape of the smile—all these trembled on the edge of recognition and slipped away. She had known so many men, but all had died . . . .

"Not all," he said.

"You're . . . . " She gasped as recognition flooded in. "David! But all this . . . . " She placed her palm against his massive chest, stroked the clean line of his jaw. "And your voice . . . . Of course I know how it happened, since I went through it. But how did you become Van Diemann?"

"Well, I found Carrick's name on the Visitor's register at the fort. Maybe he picked Margaret up and took her to Van Diemann, or maybe he just arranged a meeting. Anyway, Carrick led me to Van Diemann. I spent almost a year out there—" He waved at the barren landscape "—living on lizards and cactus and insects. A dozen girls were brought in and their bodies dragged off to be picked clean by buzzards, before I got a chance to catch Van Diemann in the act of . . . feeding."

"And what did you do with Van Diemann?"

"Well, the arrangements he'd made were pretty good. After all, he'd been operating for two hundred years without detection. So I just left things as they were—except that instead of working for himself, Van Diemann fronts for me."

"You mean Webb is really Van Diemann?"

"Yes. He's been under control too long to shift for himself. He's little more than a zombie—a thinking zombie, but without a will of his own."

"And Carrick? Was he looking for me?"

"I alerted everyone. Carrick is one of a half-dozen scouts Van Diemann was using."

"Betraying his own people—"

"He didn't know Van Diemann wasn't human."

"But he knew the girls died!"

"Well yes. That bothers him. Eventually he'll commit suicide, but meanwhile he's a conscientious worker. I can't say the same about the one I left at your mother's to watch for you. He didn't know you were there until after you'd gone." He stooped down and picked up her towel, then draped it over her shoulders. "Let's go inside, before you get cold."

She felt her excitement rise when they entered his room. He undressed, his body highlighted by the red glow of the desert sky. She loved the flat double planes of his upper chest, the ridged perfection of his stomach, the long clean golden triangle of his torso. As they lay together on the silken sheet, she drew a deep breath and pressed herself against him. "I feel fluttery. Like it's my wedding night." She gasped as she felt his hard stallion rigidity probing. "Is this the way we do it?"

"Do you know of another way?"

"Oh. No. No." The question had become meaningless, for he was inside her and it felt so good and holy that her heart ached. Each movement was a sigh of perfumed air in a sultan's garden, each touch a note of music pulsing along her nerves. She seemed to be climbing a mountain, out of a valley of slime. Soon she would reach the top, Nirvana, Heaven . . . .

Suddenly David stopped moving. For a moment her actions continued, like an engine that turns over after the switch is off. Then she became aware that his weight had gone inert, like cold mutton. The temperature of his skin, a moment ago like sun-warmed stone, had become neutral. His eyes—she twisted her neck to look, and her jaws gaped open, locked in a soundless scream.

His eyes were not eyes but painted glass. Not that they had ceased to see; they had never seen. The lovely body was not dead; it had never lived.

In a frenzy she pushed herself from beneath him and leaped out of bed. Her skin tried to crawl off her body. She sensed a presence behind her which raised each single hair on her head, drew each cell of her flesh into a knot of cold fear.

She turned.

It lay in the fireplace, a mass of gray writhings. It made a dry whispering sound as its gray thousand-tentacled shape spread out across the hearth. It came nearer, not exactly moving, but rather as though its mass had filled the cavity of the fireplace and was spreading into the room.

Ageless, eternal, utterly loathsome. She screamed, and the sound ripped apart the veils of deceit she had so carefully wrapped around herself. Hate exploded inside her brain, burning away all fear. The thing was Evil. It had planted its seed in her. Ah, when? So many years ago at the fort on that strange cricket-chirruping afternoon . . . so tiny at first, like a spider inside her brain; as the years passed it invaded her body like a million gray maggots until she was so completely consumed by evil that she didn't know.

She shrieked with rage and lunged at the shape which now covered most of the floor. She stamped it with her bare feet, her mouth spraying spittle as she uttered the foulest obscenities she could think of. A tendril slid around her ankle and climbed her leg, entering . . . . *Oh God, no!* Another encircled her waist, hot, dry, slick like the surface of mothwings. She clawed it with her fingernails, but it seemed only to swell and grow, pulsating with pleasure. She screamed as it enwrapped her neck and forced its way between her jaws. Even then she did not surrender, but clamped her teeth on the rubbery substance and ground them from side to side.

Swelling with contentment, the creature fed silently on the ripened fruit. The white body of Anne was visible here and there, still struggling in the coils. After a time her head appeared, its blue eyes shining, its perfect white teeth exposed in the rictus of death.

The creature began to divide itself, and then there were two.

Anne, he said, *you're beautiful.*

His coils seemed to pulse and swirl. Bright glittering streams of diamonds trickled out from his brain center and sprayed from each tentacle tip. In the infra-red spectrum, a network of hexagonal gears began to spin and shoot off emerald bursts of plasmic color. She felt the soft nudge of his communicator tentacle, sensed the warm interpenetration of cilia. Into her emotional organs flowed a quiet affirmation, delicious lethargy . . . .

Yes David. I feel the same way. But how can I feel like myself, when I can look over there and see my body—so pulpy and puffy and white?

They look that way because we are in this form.

This is the way we really are?

We are manifest only for this purpose. The creature is one; when we mate, we cease to be ourselves and merge with the One. You know.

Yes, but I don't understand. David, let's do it again . . .

The orgasm destroyed all sense of self and brought the flooding realization that her unity was not with David alone but with the whole of her race, dating back to the time when her ancestors strayed into the rarefied upper atmosphere of the ocean—long before man's forebears walked on two legs—and found the winds of the upper sea so harsh and savage that their bodies were blown apart. In time they learned to project an energy-body (for in the lower depths only electricity moved) and to sustain these bodies with energy drawn from creatures of the surface world. Ultimately there was no need to return to the depths, so the species remained in the world of light and fed on the apelike animals it inhabited. Only at the peak of passion was their energy strong enough to provide a meal, and so the history of man became a chronicle of blood and passion, love and death.

"But these people are our creatures," said Anne, brushing her hair in the bathroom. The post-coital change had been painless; she'd felt her new body grow lighter as vital energy flowed back into her flesh. Finally the tentacled form had faded and disappeared. "Shouldn't we help them?"

"Help them how?" David sat on the edge of the bathtub smoking a cigarette—a habit he'd been forced to drop after his injury, but now enjoyed again. "Several thousand years ago one of us caused one of them to pick up a rock to defend us. Pretty soon everybody had rocks. So one of us decided to protect his carrier by having him invent a sharpened stick. Before you knew it, everybody carried a spear. For centuries we had a monopoly on telepathy; now they're all starting it. The creatures mimic everything, and they breed like flies. The only thing we can do for them is to keep the herd thinned out."

"But we always take the best."

"Of course." He reached out and lightly slapped her rump. "That's natural."

"It seems . . . Evil."

"Matter of viewpoint. To the worm, a chicken is Evil. To the fox, a chicken is a delicious meal. Evil is the name we give the enemy. I wouldn't be surprised to learn that even we are not at the top of the food chain. Which reminds me . . . . " He got up and flipped his cigarette into the stool. "We'll have to go out to eat. There's not a thing in the house."

He looked at her and laughed.

AVON   NEW LEADER IN SCIENCE FICTION

SCIENCE FICTION HALL OF FAME

The Greatest Science Fiction Stories of All Time
Edited by Robert Silverberg
Chosen by the Members of The Science Fiction Writers of America
"Definitive! if ever lives up to its subtitle."
—LESTER DEL REY

672 pages $1.50

The greatest science fiction stories of all time chosen by the Science Fiction Writers of America.

"DEFINITIVE!"
Lester del Rey

"A BASIC ONE-VOLUME LIBRARY OF THE SHORT SCIENCE FICTION STORY."
Algis Budrys